"Why are you being so nice to us?"

Sharpe clutched his chest over his heart dramatically. "You wound me."

"That came out wrong," Emma said, her cheeks turning the color of a ripe tomato. "It's just that you have to admit it would have been so much easier for you to take my money. Instead, you offered to spend time with my brother, even after he destroyed your poor pumpkins."

He shrugged. "I guess I see a lot of myself in Aidan. I got into a fair bit of trouble of my own when I was his age. I just thought I could help him, show him what it means to be responsible."

"Well, thank you. I believe if anyone can handle Aidan, you can," Emma said. She captured his gaze with hers. "He already appears to respect you."

He didn't have the slightest idea what to say to her. He really felt for Emma. It took courage to suddenly step in as a guardian when she hadn't even known she had a brother.

And for some reason, which he still couldn't put his finger on, he wanted to help her.

Maybe it was a God thing.

Or maybe he was just losing his good sense.

A *Publishers Weekly* bestselling and award-winning author of over forty novels, **Deb Kastner** enjoys writing Western stories set in small communities. Deb lives in beautiful Colorado with her husband. She is blessed with three adult daughters and two grandchildren. Her favorite hobby is spoiling her grandchildren, but she also enjoys reading, watching movies, singing in the church choir and exploring the Rocky Mountains on horseback.

Visit the Author Profile page at LoveInspired.com for more titles.

A Reason to Stay

Deb Kastner

LOVE INSPIRED
INSPIRATIONAL ROMANCE

LOVE INSPIRED®
INSPIRATIONAL ROMANCE

Recycling programs
for this product may
not exist in your area.

ISBN-13: 978-1-335-58598-1

A Reason to Stay

Love Inspired
22 Adelaide St. West, 41st Floor
Toronto, Ontario M5H 4E3, Canada
www.LoveInspired.com

Printed in U.S.A.

And the Lord God said,
It is not good that the man should be alone;
I will make an help meet for him.
—*Genesis* 2:18

To my granddaughter Isabella and in memory of her border collie, Baloo. You continue to amaze me with your intelligence, kindness and strength as you grow into a lovely young lady.

I'm so proud of you!

Chapter One

Up until this moment, Emma Fitzpatrick had surprisingly been enjoying her day at the Colorado mountain country Harvest Festival, much more than she'd expected, since country *anything* wasn't her cup of tea in the least. The local park was covered in hues of glittering reds and golds from the aspen trees and muted evergreen from lodgepole pines. Country music boomed from a local band playing on a platform that had been erected in the middle of the town park. The entire town—the entire state, for that matter—had gone from green to gold in the blink of an eye, and Emma couldn't fail to be moved by God's natural beauty.

Whispering Pines, Colorado, was a great deal different from Chicago, where she'd been born and raised, and even more so LA, where she currently lived.

Her grandmother had asked her and her younger brother, Aidan, to accompany her to the town's annual Harvest Festival on the first Saturday in October. Thanks to her father's estrangement from his mother, Emma hadn't been allowed any contact with Nan growing up. And it was especially important to her to spend time with her now. Nan had said she wanted to meet up with *friends*, but due to her fading vision, she couldn't drive herself, and there was no rideshare service or a taxi in such a small town.

Emma couldn't very well say no to her adorably begging Nan, so here they were at the fair—although her feisty eighty-year-old nan had long since deserted her for the company of a beaming man around Nan's age.

Friends, indeed.

Nan and the handsome old gentleman had their heads together and looked as if they were high schoolers on their first date, smiling and laughing loud enough for those nearby to hear.

Emma would have rolled her eyes if it wasn't so cute.

Instead, she adjusted the light rust-colored scarf Nan had knitted her and joined a small group of women all in their mid-to late twenties, including her new friend Ruby Winslow, whom she'd met the other day in town at Sally's Pizza when she'd been picking up dinner for Nan and Aidan.

Relaxing into the moment as she chatted with her new friends, she wasn't paying attention to the noises around her until her ears picked up the sound of skirmishing boys and recognized the still only slightly familiar voice of her nine-year-old brother, Aidan.

This past week had given her the biggest shock of her entire twenty-nine-year life. Not only did she *have* a brother she hadn't known existed, but she had discovered she was his legal guardian.

Emma looked over to see what was going on.

"Leave me alone," Aidan growled, his face flushed with anger and nearly as red as his curly hair. Though his tone was high and tight, his words didn't sound like a plea so much as a rough demand.

Four much older boys, probably all in their late teens, hovered over Aidan, who, though small and gangly compared to the boys around him, puffed out his chest and lifted his chin in response, not backing down despite his smaller size.

"You little twerp," said a large boy with white-blond hair, poking his finger at Aidan's chest. "Look at you, tough guy. You wanna fight with me?"

"Oh, no," Emma murmured as she watched the brawl unfolding before her, knowing she should do something but feeling frozen to the spot.

She didn't know how to take care of her brother.

She didn't even *know* her brother.

The older boy laughed and pushed Aidan in the chest with both hands, sending him sprawling backward into the dirt.

Aidan quickly regained his footing. Before the blond boy even realized what was happening, Aidan scrambled to his feet and shoved his shoulder into the boy's gut, following it with a strong left hook that landed high on the boy's cheek. The kid was definitely going to have a shiner from the exchange, and Emma cringed.

Emma's limbs loosened, and she rushed

forward, calling Aidan's name, knowing she was already too late to undo the damage her brother had created. As her brother's newly appointed guardian, she was now accountable for him and knew it was up to her to step up to the plate and take responsibility for his actions. But breaking up the young boys' fight was entirely out of her comfort zone, not to mention her experience.

She combed nervous fingers back through her pixie-cut auburn hair, puffing out a visible breath in the cool, crisp fall air as she wondered if she should—or even could—cut into the middle of the skirmish. She was only five-two, and three out of the four teenage boys were taller and broader than she was.

Thankfully, at that moment, a dark-haired cowboy Emma didn't recognize took it upon himself to step into the fray. Emma wondered if he was any of the boys' father.

"Knock it off, guys," the man said calmly, holding out his hands between the two scrapping young men. The other boys in the group, those not directly involved with the fight, quickly dispersed, backing away from the tall, scowling man.

Emma couldn't blame them for making

themselves scarce. The cowboy was quite intimidating, with his broad shoulders and black cowboy hat pulled low over narrowed ice-blue eyes.

"Brandon, you're better than this," he told the blond boy in a gruff, low voice. "If your daddy catches you fighting again, you know he's gonna take your cell phone away from you for the rest of the year."

Emma absorbed the cowboy's words, trying to make sense of them. First, the man apparently didn't have any skin in the game, as she'd first suspected, which made her especially grateful that he'd stepped in to help. He wasn't anyone's father—at least, none of the scrapping boys'.

Also, it was clear this wasn't Brandon's first tussle. It had appeared to Emma that the young man had been the one picking the fight against Aidan, but there was no way to know for sure.

She had no idea whether or not her broody little brother had the tendency to get into scuffles. From what little she knew of him, he preferred to spend his time alone playing video games or coding on his computer, which in truth came as no real surprise to her. Video games were probably Aidan's way of escaping the real world—somewhere that had probably been as bad for him as the reality she'd fled from when she'd turned eighteen.

Aidan would have felt equally trapped, as she honestly didn't believe her parents would have changed much since she'd broken all contact with them. From what little she'd learned from Aidan, he'd grown up in the same situation as she had. Their father was hardly a decent role model, having been one way in public and much different behind closed doors. Their mother wasn't much better. Emma had never been allowed to know her grandmother. And according to Aidan, it had been likewise with him.

Emma had escaped to the West Coast the moment she'd turned eighteen. She hadn't looked back since.

Until now.

She'd worked hard for a full scholarship to Stanford, then had taken a job at a major marketing firm in LA—until she'd received the totally unexpected call that had immediately sent her world into a tailspin.

She jerked herself from the past and turned her attention back to the scene before her.

The teenager Brandon had immediately

dropped his gaze at the cowboy's gruff words, looking at the ground and scuffing his cowboy boots in the dirt. "Yeah. I know. Please don't say anything to my dad." The tough boy's voice was suddenly a squeaky, high-pitched whine now that all his friends had deserted him.

"I suggest you go find the other kids you were hanging with and stay out of trouble for once. Oh—and leave the new kid alone."

"Yeah, okay," Brandon said again, this time using the cowboy's words as an excuse to exit the scene as fast as he could, bolting off at a dead run.

The cowboy then turned to address Aidan, but Emma's brother had surprisingly disappeared into the crowd and was nowhere to be seen.

Emma's gaze had been focused on the interaction between the man and Brandon, and she hadn't seen which direction her brother had gone. Her anxiety increased exponentially with every passing second. Her heart was pounding out of her chest.

She belatedly wished she had followed her original instincts and skipped the festival altogether, no matter how much Nan had pressed her. Aidan hadn't wanted to go, and she shouldn't have dragged him out the door with him complaining the whole way.

She shouldn't have forced his acquiescence—at least, not until she knew him better. How could she have known he had a propensity for fighting?

Emma rejoined the small group of women she'd been chatting with earlier, her gut churning with apprehension and adrenaline pulsing through her veins.

"Aidan took off," Emma said, her voice lined with worry. "I'd better go see if I can find him before he gets into even more trouble."

"We'll help," Ruby replied. "My five siblings are hanging around here somewhere. I'll give everyone a quick text and ask them to be on the lookout for Aidan. Between all of us, we ought to be able to find him in no time. Don't worry, Emma. It'll be okay."

"I appreciate it," Emma replied, her gloved hands curling into fists. It wasn't so much that she was concerned for Aidan's safety. Whispering Pines was a small, friendly mountain town with an almost nonexistent crime rate. She was more worried about what Aidan could do to Whispering Pines if given the opportunity. He'd already shown his penchant for creating trouble.

"Give me a minute to gather my peeps," Ruby said.

Ruby was as good as her word, and within minutes, all five of her adult siblings were gathered around, three smiling women and two handsome men—including, to Emma's surprise, the dark-haired cowboy who'd broken up the fight earlier. Though the Winslow siblings had various combinations of hair and eye colors, all six were clearly related, with strong facial features and clefts in their chins.

"I appreciate everyone being willing to help look for my brother. Aidan is nine years old and almost as tall as I am," she started, holding up her hand to gesture the boy's height. "He's skinny and has a mop of curly red hair and blue eyes."

Knowing a picture was worth a thousand words, Emma brought up on her phone a photo she'd taken of Aidan and showed the picture around, her chest tightening as she forced a breath of biting mountain air into her lungs. Colorado's dry, crisp autumn air was unlike any she'd ever experienced before.

"How do you want to go about this?" the

cowboy she'd seen earlier asked in a low, rich but husky baritone. "As far as I'm concerned, the sooner we find this kid, the better."

Emma's gaze widened in surprise at the unspoken but blatantly clear message—better *for me*.

While Ruby's brother's statement could have indicated that he was worried about Aidan, Emma thought it sounded more as if he felt she was taking him away from something he considered a more important use of his time.

What could possibly be more important than finding a missing child?

"Sharpe, don't be such a jerk," Ruby said, slapping her brother on his shoulder.

So Emma had been right.

This cowboy, *Sharpe*, was more concerned about his own schedule than he was about Aidan. And yet, earlier, he'd taken the time out of his obviously busy schedule to break up the fight between the boys. The disparity was a bit baffling.

Sharpe shrugged. "I didn't say I *wouldn't* search for the boy. Can I help it if all of you get to play around and enjoy the festival while I have work to do?" He didn't sound bitter, just matter-of-fact. "I'm just saying we need to get this done as fast as possible so I can get back to selling my pumpkins."

"As you can see, I've got plenty of help here to assist me in my search," Emma said to Sharpe, feeling her ire rising at his cavalier attitude, knowing and not particularly caring that it showed in her voice. "Please feel free to go back to whatever you were doing that is clearly so important to you." Emma couldn't help but slip in that last part.

Despite the composed way he'd handled the fight between the boys earlier and her gratefulness for him stepping in for Aidan so her brother hadn't gotten seriously hurt, now that he was here with the other adults, she immediately rather disliked this man. He had *arrogant* written all over him.

Sharpe grunted and crossed his arms over his chest, highlighting his biceps, to Emma's dismay. She'd always been a big fan of well-built biceps, but *not* when they were attached to blatantly rude men. She shifted her gaze back to his frowning face.

"Well, I'm here now. Let's get this done." Sharpe pushed his words through in a gruff monotone.

"Do we need a plan of action as to who is

going to search where?" a blonde Winslow sister who introduced herself as Avery asked. "I suggest we spread out. Half of us can go toward the north side of the festival area and half toward the south. I doubt Aidan will have wandered out much farther than the festival perimeter. There are way too many interesting things that would no doubt capture a boy's interest going on at the fair for him to have completely left the area."

Emma half wanted to disagree with Avery's words. From what little she knew of Aidan, she wasn't sure a country fair would interest her brother. He was used to city life, where festivals had roller coasters and spinning teacups and famous bands, not games like trying to throw a ring over a bottle or a dart at a balloon. Just this morning, Aidan had complained about having to accompany her, saying he'd rather stay home and play video games than go to some stupid hick festival.

And now he was proving his point.

For all Emma knew, Aidan could be anywhere, and he'd already gotten into trouble once today. Maybe he'd taken off down Main Street and was halfway back to Nan's house by now—if he knew the way to Nan's house, which Emma wasn't sure he did. That only made her even more nervous, and her throat tightened as her anxiety rose once again.

"I'll check the food tent," said Frost, the other Winslow brother, who, unlike broody Sharpe, was wearing a smile that matched his chipper, welcoming attitude. "When I was nine years old, that's exactly where I would have gone first."

"That's *still* where you go first thing," Ruby pointed out with a chuckle.

Sharpe grunted in agreement, not nearly as amused as his sister appeared to be at his brother's antics, but Frost ignored his brother and grinned nonetheless, patting his trim stomach for emphasis.

Despite the gravity of the situation, Emma appreciated the easy banter between the Winslow siblings. She'd grown up as an only child and had always longed for a brother or sister.

But now that she suddenly had one, she had no idea what to do with him.

She felt as if life had just knocked her on the side of the head with a steel pipe and tossed her into the Pacific Ocean.

She was in way over her head. She couldn't breathe, and if she wasn't careful, she was likely to drown.

Sharpe had a ton of work to do to prepare for selling his wares at the Harvest Festival. It had taken him longer than expected to load the flatbed with pumpkins, gourds and autumn grasses and wreaths this morning, and because he'd taken time out of his morning to break up the boys getting into that fistfight, he hadn't even raised his canopy for the sale yet. He was going to be at least an hour late in preparing to sell everything he'd brought.

He hated being late.

And now he was going to be even later because of the search for some kid who couldn't manage to stay out of trouble. Maybe he was second-guessing the trouble part, but he'd already broken up a fight in which the boy had been involved, and now the young man had evidently slipped off without letting his sister know where he was going.

As far as Sharpe was concerned, that sounded like trouble, and he should know. He recognized it from his own youth. Sharpe had been a handful at Aidan's age, and he remembered that sneaking off without telling anyone where you were going was never a good thing.

Then again, there were already more than half a dozen adults looking for the kid, and the festival—the whole town, for that matter—wasn't that large. Feeling the crisis was well in hand, he decided to return to his flatbed and start unloading his pumpkins, gourds and the autumn leaf wreaths his sisters had made by hand, which he intended to sell at the festival. While many customers enjoyed visiting Winslow's Woodlands because the farm offered so much more than merely selling landscaping materials—a sleigh ride in the winter or hayrack ride in the summer, a petting zoo, ice-skating, or fishing in the pond—he still liked to man a booth at the Harvest Festival.

He usually did fairly well selling his pumpkins at the festival, when people were in the mood to spend money. At the very least, he was always able to hand out plenty of flyers advertising the family businesses—Winslow's Woodlands Christmas tree farm and A New Leash on Love service dog program—

and drum up interest from potential customers and clients.

He was the salesman of the family, though not because he was a people person. Compared to his outgoing brother and sisters, he was more of a loner, and given his druthers, he preferred to keep to himself. But when his parents had passed away when he was sixteen, as the oldest sibling, he hadn't had any choice but to take the family reins. Winslow's would have tanked without him. So he'd thrown himself into his family's Christmas tree farm and landscaping business and learned all he could through books and webinars about selling and managing a business and encouraged his brother and sisters to follow their dreams.

Just before he'd broken up the fight between the boys on the green, he'd backed the flatbed up to the spot he'd been given to set up his booth. He'd been in the middle of setting out the poles and stretching the canopy when he'd received the SOS text from Ruby to help find Aidan.

Now that he'd decided *not* to participate in that particular game of hide-and-seek, he returned to his canopy—or rather, the poles and canvas laid out on the ground waiting for him to assemble. He figured he could keep his eyes out for the boy while he was working in case any of his sisters got on his case about it.

Raising a large canopy wasn't easy on his own, but he'd done it enough times that he knew how to stake the ground and in what order to put up the poles. It would only take him a moment to set up the few rectangular tables he'd brought along on which to display his wares. The bigger job was going to be getting his flatbed of pumpkins unloaded.

As he worked, he hummed along with the live country music blaring from the festival platform. Whispering Pines festivals weren't really his thing, but hawking his pumpkins was. By God's grace, he would completely sell out today and be able to add a big chunk of change to the family business coffers.

Even over his humming and the music from the loudspeakers, as he approached his truck to start unloading his pumpkins, he couldn't miss the sudden, distinct screech of a cell phone playing one of those videos all the kids seemed to like these days. And if he wasn't mistaken, the sound was coming from the back of his flatbed.

It figures.

Sharpe frowned when he discovered the missing boy, who had crawled over dozens of pumpkins and gourds and was now spread out over the homemade leaf wreaths his sisters had made. Not surprisingly, his nose was in his phone, and Sharpe's ire rose when he realized Aidan had not even bothered to move the homemade wreaths and ribboned grass bundles out of the way.

The only Winslow not actively looking for the boy had to be the one to find him.

"Aidan, is it?" Sharpe barked as he clenched his fists at his sides and worked to even his pitch. This kid had just stomped all over his pumpkins with his jagged-edged cowboy boots and ruined at least a half a pallet of pumpkins.

The boy jumped at the sound of his name, and his gaze widened when he realized it was Sharpe speaking to him.

"Who's asking?" Aidan growled back defiantly, despite the expression on his face that suggested he didn't actually want to have anything to do with Sharpe.

"I suggest you lose the attitude, young man." Sharpe scowled at the boy. He wasn't in the mood for this. Not after everything else that had gone wrong this morning. "You're already in a lot of trouble as it is. Your sister is looking for you. And don't even try to act as if you don't know that, since you're holding your phone in your hand and I know she's repeatedly texted you and tried calling."

Aidan just shrugged, as if Sharpe's words meant nothing to him, and returned his attention to his phone screen.

What did he think? That if he ignored Sharpe the man would go away?

Sharpe pulled his own cell phone out of his pocket and texted Ruby that he'd found the boy near his truck and asked for Emma to come get him ASAP. He didn't mention that Aidan had smashed pumpkins and other items in his flatbed. That was his own problem to solve. He didn't want to put that on Emma. It was hardly her fault her brother was misbehaving. She already had her hands full just trying to take care of the sullen young man.

In the meantime, Sharpe decided to act, starting with getting the kid out of the truck, hopefully without doing any more damage than had already been done.

How to do that was another question entirely.

Less than a minute later, his sister Ruby approached with Aidan's sister, Emma, at her heel, worry creasing her face.

Sharpe couldn't help but give her a quick once-over. The woman's outfit was a far cry from what the ladies around here wore to a country festival and was entirely impractical in every way. He suspected Emma's black woolen peacoat and designer slacks probably cost more than he made in a month, and she was wearing high-heeled, knee-high, black leather boots instead of anything remotely sensible. The boots looked like something that belonged on a runway, not at a festival. Still, she somehow managed to remain upright and square-shouldered, confidently striding around on her heels without the least bit of wobble to her step.

As Emma approached, she appeared relieved to have found Aidan, for all of about two seconds—until she saw where her brother was and what he'd done to the pumpkins and wreaths in the flatbed. Sharpe didn't point out the obvious, because he could clearly see the dismay written all over her face as she took in the scene before her.

"Aidan. Get out of that truck *now*," Emma demanded, clenching her fists against her hips.

Aidan glared at Emma and didn't move an inch except to shove his curly red hair off his forehead and lift his phone to the level of his eyes to intentionally ignore Emma.

"You need to listen to your sister," Sharpe added, backing up Emma's words with his own stern tone. "Out of the truck, kid. Now."

If anything, that only made the boy dig in his proverbial heels, which made Sharpe worry even more about the state of his pumpkins. Aidan was clearly angry at being ganged up on and was balking at the notion of being told what to do. The stubborn tilt of his chin told Sharpe everything he needed to know. He well remembered his own youth and how his encounters with adults had often left him irate and moody.

His brow low over his bright blue eyes, a scowling Aidan reluctantly stood. Sharpe held his breath, expecting the young man to purposefully stomp over more of his pumpkins on his way off the truck, but instead Aidan turned and deftly leaped over the side, landing squarely on his feet like a cat.

Sharpe surveyed the overall damage to his pumpkins and wreaths. Some of the pumpkins and gourds, especially those where Aidan had hopped into the back of the truck, had been completely smashed and were beyond repair, but thankfully most of his stock had survived.

"Give me your phone," Emma demanded, holding out one hand to her brother, palm up, while keeping the other fisted on her hip.

"No." Aidan curled his phone close to his chest.

Emma raised her eyebrows and continued to hold her hand out. There was a long moment of tense silence, but in the end, it was enough. She didn't say another word before Aidan grudgingly complied and dropped the phone into her hand with a growl of protest.

Emma turned to his text messages and held the screen right in front of Aidan's face. "Do you *see* how many texts I sent you? Phone calls, too, Aidan. I know you were playing with your phone, so don't you even try to tell me you weren't looking directly at the screen.

You had to have seen that I was trying to get ahold of you. Why didn't you answer me?"

He shrugged and looked at the ground. "Just didn't feel like it."

Emma sighed in exasperation. "That is *not* a good answer."

Sharpe, who usually didn't intrude in matters that weren't his business, wanted to step in, but only because he could see both sides of the issue. He remembered back when he was a boy how he'd purposefully infuriate the adults around him because he'd believed they didn't understand him. Now, looking at the other side of the coin was equally fascinating. Through his sister Ruby, Sharpe knew a bit about Emma's circumstances—and knew she'd been introduced to her little brother for the first time only days ago.

"Because of you, a lot of people had to take time away from enjoying their day in order to look for you when you took off like that. That was unkind, Aidan. You need to learn to think about how other people feel instead of just what you want. Because of your behavior today, you've lost your phone privileges for the rest of the day."

"Emma," Aidan whined, crossing his arms,

his face flushing with heat Sharpe guessed was a combination of anger and embarrassment at being called out in front of strangers. His cheeks were flaming as red as his hair. "That's not fair."

"Go get in the car and wait for me there," Emma demanded, pointing in the direction of the parking lot. "I'll have to find Nan and let her know we're leaving. We'll discuss what's *fair* when we get back to the house."

Emma let out another sigh as she watched Aidan stomp off, then turned to Sharpe, meeting his gaze square on. She had beautiful copper penny–colored eyes, the kind a man could melt in. But it was a quick thought and only in passing. Her expression was far too serious for Sharpe to do more than equally meet her gaze and wait for her to speak.

"I'm so sorry for all the damage my brother has done." She reached into her no doubt extremely expensive purse—the kind with a brand name Sharpe didn't recognize scrawled across the outside—and withdrew a wallet with the initials ESF engraved on it.

Sharpe vaguely wondered what the *S* stood for as she opened it and removed a business card. She riffled through her purse again and withdrew a purple ink pen, popping the top off with her teeth and writing something in large, loopy handwriting on the back of the card.

"My cell phone number is on the front and is usually the best way to get ahold of me, but this is the number of the landline where I'm staying while we're in town," she said, holding out the card to him. "At my nan's house."

He took it and glanced at the local number. He was familiar with her grandmother, as they attended the same church, and he knew where she lived, Whispering Pines being such a small town and all.

But why was Emma giving him her phone number?

Heat rose into his face, and he was glad for the scruff that covered most of his cheeks—because the first thing that had flashed into his mind was that she was asking him for a date.

"I—I… What's this for?" he stammered, then lowered his brow. He was acting like a schoolboy with his first crush just because Emma was a pretty woman, and he was confused.

If Emma noticed, she gave no indication of it.

"Add up the damage and call me with what

I owe you for it," she stated in a calm, cool voice.

She wanted to give him money.

That realization only made his face heat even more, but this time for a different reason. How could he even have considered that she might want to date him?

"I don't think—" he started, but she cut him off with a wave of her hand.

"Please. It's the least I can do for all the trouble Aidan caused you. I can see he ruined many of your pumpkins. And look at all the lovely wreaths he's destroyed."

Maybe that was true, but how was the kid ever going to learn a lesson if his sister simply wrote a check for the damage he'd done, digging him out every time he got in trouble?

Not only that, but Sharpe didn't really want to take her money. It didn't feel right in his gut—and he always listened to his gut.

He rocked back on the heels of his cowboy boots and crossed his arms. "Thanks for the offer, Emma, but I've got a better idea."

Chapter Two

Emma had to admit Sharpe's idea might really be better—for Aidan.

For her, not so much.

Neither, she thought, was it really going to be better for Sharpe—or at least it wouldn't be nearly as straightforward as taking a check from her would have been. Why he thought he needed to teach Aidan a lesson was beyond Emma. Aidan certainly wasn't Sharpe's problem.

But the large, looming cowboy had been bullheaded and, frankly, more than a little intimidating. He wouldn't take her money, and that was all there was to it. She'd tried to argue the point so he'd see the easy way out, but he wouldn't hear of it. Rather, he'd suggested Aidan learn a *real* lesson about destroying other people's property by working off what he owed for the pumpkins at Winslow's Woodlands.

Truthfully, Emma would just as soon have paid for the damage and called it a day. It would have been far simpler for her. With her parents' recent deaths in a car accident, she was her parents' estate manager, as well as her brother's new permanent legal guardian, and she felt as if she was in over her head sorting out their affairs while at the same time trying to figure out how she was going to take her brother back to California with her when her extended family leave ended just after Thanksgiving.

It was a lot to think about.

Too much, really, to be on her shoulders when she had no one else to depend on. She was totally alone in this.

Before, that was how she'd liked it—alone and free to make her own decisions.

Now she didn't have a choice.

Nor did she have an option as to whether or not to accompany Aidan to the Winslows' for his afternoon *lesson* on how not to disrespect other people's property. But there was no way she was about to drop him off for Sharpe to deal with on his own, especially not after all the mischief Aidan had already gotten into the previous Saturday. What would happen if Aidan threw his attitude at Sharpe?

She had the sinking feeling that, perhaps without realizing it, Sharpe had just bitten off more than he could chew with her brother. Then again, Sharpe was obviously level-headed and practical—exactly what a boy like Aidan needed right now.

Still, she couldn't imagine why Sharpe had even suggested such an exchange. After all, he'd now have to spend his own time and energy on Aidan, which Emma couldn't help but think would slow Sharpe down with whatever he was doing.

Why hadn't he just taken the money?

A twinge of guilt skittered up the back of her neck.

She should be grateful.

Sharpe was investing in her little brother, and she had no idea why.

"You are to do *exactly* as Sharpe asks you," she told her brother as she pulled into the parking lot at Winslow's Woodlands. "No complaining. No backtalking. Do you understand me?"

Aidan merely stared out the passenger-side window of her black sedan and grunted his assent.

"I'm serious, Aidan. No matter what he asks you to do, you'll do it. Muck stalls, scrub down his tools. Whatever he wants. Are we clear?"

She didn't even get a grunt this time, and she sighed inwardly in frustration. She honestly had no idea what to do with this broody young boy with a chip on his shoulder.

"Let's go," she said, then exited the vehicle, waiting for Aidan to do the same. Her feet immediately hit gravel and she slid in the ballet flats she'd selected to wear that day. Better than the heels she'd worn to the autumn festival by far, but still not good enough for this kind of terrain. She made a mental note to visit town and invest in better shoes for mountain walking.

Sharpe had evidently been watching for Aidan, because he immediately approached them, an energetic border collie at his heels.

"Emma. Aidan. Good to see you both."

Emma nodded, her throat suddenly too dry to speak.

"Cool. A dog," Aidan muttered, suddenly in

a hurry to exit the sedan. "What's her name?" He knelt by the dog and laughed when it barked and licked his cheek.

"*His* name is Blue. He's a border collie. We keep quite a variety of breeds of dogs around here, what with A New Leash on Love, our service dog training program, also on Winslow property. But Blue here is my own personal dog."

Ruby had told Emma about the Winslows' other business. She and some of her sisters trained service dogs for a number of purposes. Emma had never owned a dog herself, living in a no-pets-allowed high-rise apartment in LA.

"Baloo," Aidan repeated, lengthening the syllables. "Cool. Just like the bear in *The Jungle Book*."

Emma chuckled. Aidan had privately told her *The Jungle Book* was his favorite movie, and he'd watched it more than once in the past couple of weeks, singing along with all the songs. It warmed Emma's heart, since Aidan was trying in so many ways to grow up. She hoped he'd maintain this little piece of his childhood.

Still, Aidan had misheard Sharpe.

"No, Aidan, I think Sharpe said his dog's name is—" she started, but Sharpe held up a hand to cut her off.

"Baloo," Sharpe said, likewise lengthening the syllables as he winked at Emma, "is a certified therapy dog. I take him with me to homeless shelters and hospitals. Every service dog has a job, and his is to cheer people up."

"Really? Cool. Could we come with you sometime and watch him work?"

Sharpe's questioning gaze turned to Emma. She didn't think Aidan even knew what he was asking, and it was far beyond anything she'd ever experienced.

Visit a homeless shelter? A hospital, maybe. Then again, it might open his eyes to the world around him.

"It'll be good for him," Sharpe assured her. "I visit a homeless veterans' shelter most Saturdays. Maybe we can set something up."

She shrugged and nodded at Sharpe. She'd hoped he'd lean toward a hospital rather than a homeless shelter, but that, she realized, was due to her own discomfort. These were people who'd been injured while bravely serving their country on her behalf.

And to think all this had started because Aidan had trampled Sharpe's pumpkins.

"Okay. We'll sit down together later and figure out a time to go visiting. Aidan, have you ever ridden a horse before?"

Aidan's eyes widened, and he shook his head.

"Are you up for it?"

Her brother swallowed hard and nodded, but Emma wasn't convinced. The kid looked terrified.

"I—er…" she stammered, stepping into Sharpe's line of vision.

He pulled off his cowboy hat and pressed the fabric of his shirt on his arm to his forehead. "Yeah?"

"I'd hoped to be able to stay for the afternoon and, well, you know…"

She wasn't sure how to finish that sentence, so she didn't.

"Watch over my shoulder?" he suggested.

"No," she squeaked, heat rising into her face. "That's not what I meant at all. It's just that I don't know my brother that well yet, and he's here because he got into trouble, so…"

"You want to keep an eye on him."

This man was really starting to get her

goat, the way he kept finishing her sentences for her. Even if he was right.

"Yes" was all she could think of to say.

"I can handle Aidan if you have other things to do," he offered, tilting his head down to meet her eyes. "I promise I won't leave him on his own."

"No, that's okay. If you don't mind, I'd rather stay here and watch over Aidan myself. I'm just not comfortable—"

"Leaving him with a stranger. I get it." He chuckled. "Trust me. I can handle anything the kid throws at me. I practically raised four of my siblings."

She stepped back and gave him a once-over.

"No, that's not what I was going to say. Aidan is— Well, he can really put up an attitude. More often than not, he gets bored with whatever he's doing after a few minutes, and then he'll start giving you guff. And I wouldn't want him to do that after you've been so nice to us."

"Okay."

"Okay?" She hadn't expected that, especially such a quick capitulation.

He shrugged. "I don't see why not. You

may even enjoy it. Just give me a minute and I'll get a horse tacked up for you, too."

He didn't even wait for her to agree but headed toward the barn, his border collie at one heel and a scurrying Aidan at the other.

Emma wasn't sure what she'd just signed up for, and she hesitated just outside the barn door. She'd assumed Sharpe would have Aidan doing strenuous farmwork—such as mucking out stalls. Instead, he was offering something fun.

Well, fun for Aidan, if his glowing gaze was anything to go by when Sharpe led the already-mounted young man out on a gray mare named Diamond.

Growing up in the suburbs of Chicago, Emma hadn't ever been around horses, not any more than Aidan had, and she wasn't sure she shared the young boy's enthusiasm, especially when Sharpe tied Aidan's horse to the corral fence and strode back into the barn, returning with an enormous bay.

He actually expected her to get up on that thing?

"This is Elijah," Sharpe said, running a hand down the horse's neck. "He's the gentlest gelding we have in our stable."

Emma tried to smile but had the distinct feeling it came out as more of a wince.

"Come on over," Sharpe encouraged her. "I'll give you a lift up."

At first, Emma pictured Sharpe sweeping her into his arms like some romantic hero, and her heart rate skyrocketed, so she chuckled aloud when Sharpe clasped his hands together and indicated she should put her left foot into the stirrup he'd created.

"What's so funny?" he asked as she followed his directions and swung her right leg over the horse's back. It still felt like a long way down, but once Sharpe had adjusted the saddle's stirrups to fit her size, she didn't feel quite so timid.

At least, until the horse moved and she squeaked in alarm.

Sharpe threaded the reins over Elijah's head and showed Emma how to use them. "Left means *left*, right means *right*, a little nip with your heels means *giddyap* and pulling backward on the reins means *whoa*. Got it?"

She thought she'd mostly be using the whoa signal but didn't say so. She just nodded.

Sharpe did the same for Aidan with Diamond and then mounted his own horse, a huge black that Emma thought fitted Sharpe's personality.

"Follow my lead," Sharpe instructed. "Nose to tail. The horses know what to do."

Emma hoped that was the case, because she certainly didn't. Even the dog seemed to know to come along without Sharpe calling to him.

As Sharpe led them down into the country on what looked to be a well-used path as wide as a tractor, or maybe a hayrack, she found her anxiety lessening as she rode. She didn't know whether it was the saddle's hypnotic back-and-forth rocking, the clip-clop of the horses' hooves or maybe the fresh, clean mountain breeze, but the farther they went, the more the weight of the world lifted from her shoulders. Her past with her parents, her current issues with Aidan, her uncertain future in LA and her dreams for a business of her own—all her worries seemed to just melt away until her mind was only filled with the sights, sounds and scents around her: the lodgepole pines and blue spruce mixed in with sparkling gold and yellow aspens, the birdsong weaving in and out as if in harmony with the sound of the horses' hooves, the crisp scent of evergreen and the unfamiliar yet not unpleasant smell of horse and saddle leather.

It had been far too long since she'd just *stopped.*

She'd pushed herself through a full-ride scholarship to Stanford and into the crazy-busy world of big-city marketing. She hadn't even realized places like Winslow's Woodlands existed except as a picture you'd see on a Christmas card. And while it was probably true that Sharpe worked very hard in his business, the whole mountain country town held an air of slowing down to enjoy the scenery. The people she'd met in Whispering Pines took the time to get to know each other. And from what she'd seen, the Winslows seemed especially close to one another. They worshipped together and spent recreational time in each other's company. The sisters all had spouses who happily joined in.

She didn't have any idea how she'd provide such security for her brother, but right now, with her horse, Elijah, following Diamond's tail—which allowed Emma to really enjoy the scenery—she didn't need to worry about it.

After they'd been riding for another ten

minutes, Sharpe reined in his horse next to Aidan.

"Ready to get your hands dirty?" he asked, pressing his large hand onto Aidan's shoulder. The boy stiffened and didn't reply.

Sharpe merely chuckled. "I thought so. Let's go."

He swung off the saddle with the ease of a man born into it and held Diamond's halter as Aidan scrambled off, not nearly as neatly as Sharpe but not too bad for his first time dismounting.

But when Sharpe turned to Elijah and held the gelding's halter for Emma, panic quickly returned. Getting onto the horse with Sharpe's help had been doable, but dismounting—well, it suddenly looked a long way down.

Sharpe waited a moment more, his eyebrows raised. "Need a hand?"

Her cheeks reddened. The last thing she wanted to do was admit she needed help from this man, but clearly, she did.

"Hook your hand around the saddle horn and swing your right leg over," he instructed, his voice surprisingly gentle. Then again, maybe he led newbies out on trail rides on a regular basis. She wasn't sure what Winslow's Woodlands offered its guests.

She followed his instructions and found herself standing stiffly with her left foot still in the stirrup. It still looked to her like a long way to solid ground, and she didn't want to end up tangled up in the stirrup.

Now what?

He chuckled and reached for her waist, lightly supporting her as she pulled her left foot from the stirrup and dropped to the ground.

"It gets easier with time," he assured her before turning back to Aidan.

"Have you ever picked a pumpkin from a patch?" he asked the boy.

"No," Aidan replied, his gaze looking out over the vast fields of orange.

"Well, then," Sharpe said, reaching into his saddlebag and removing a pair of gloves. "Here's a pair of gloves. You're going to need these."

Emma glanced down at a nearby pumpkin, noticing the multiple bristly spines growing from each one.

"You wouldn't happen to have an extra pair of gloves in there, would you?" she asked.

His gaze widened. "You're here to work?"

"I don't see why not. It's not going to do anyone any good for me just to stand around gawking."

A half grin crept up one side of his lips. "My kinda woman."

But just as quickly as he said it, the smile turned into a frown, and he yanked his cowboy hat down low over his eyes. He cleared his throat and said, "Let's go to work."

Embarrassment flooded through Sharpe. It wasn't like him to talk first and think later, but something about Emma got him all mixed up inside, and the words gushed out of him faster than he could bite his tongue to keep them in.

She wasn't *his kind of woman*. She was the exact *opposite* of his type of woman—if he even had one, which he didn't. But a fashion-forward city girl who couldn't even mount a horse? It was all he could do not to scoff aloud, but he managed to keep *that* sound from emanating from his lips, at least.

Though she was still wearing the wrong kind of shoes and was carrying a purse with the name brand scrawled right across the fabric so everyone would know it was the real thing, Emma was dressed more sensibly today than she'd been at the festival. Today she sported designer jeans and a well-made light green polo shirt for the mild autumn afternoon. She was still as pretty as the last time he'd seen her—when she'd been high fashion from tip to toe.

For some reason, a man who rarely felt intimidated by anything or anyone he encountered was now overwhelmed in a major way.

Normally, it didn't bother him that he was just a humble cowboy without a college degree working on a tree farm, but next to Emma he was feeling his blue-collar roots from the tip of his dusty black cowboy hat down to the heels of his worn, scuffed boots, and he was surprised to find the comparison actually pained him. This woman was some big-shot marketing manager from LA who clearly put a lot of time, effort and money into her appearance.

His thoughts made him feel itchy and uncomfortable, as if he were having an allergic reaction. Where was the Benadryl when he needed it?

And yet he found her attractive, more than

he'd expected to. She *was* pretty, no doubt about that. But he'd always believed if he ever married—and that was a big if—it would be to a woman who wasn't afraid to get her boots dirty.

Her *riding* boots. Not runway boots.

He watched Aidan toss a stick for Blue—*Baloo*—and laugh when the dog immediately returned it and dropped it at his feet, barking merrily.

He remembered those carefree childhood days, but they'd been gone in a snap. Sharpe was stuck in this life. He'd never had the option to be able to make any choices about what he would be or where his life would go. The moment his parents had died, he'd accepted that his life would be consumed with taking care of his younger siblings and Winslow's Woodlands.

Aidan was more like Sharpe than the boy knew. Sharpe had been sixteen when his own parents had died in an automobile accident, and he'd had to step up, along with his sister Avery, and take care of his family and the farm. He'd had to grow up in the blink of an eye, and he knew that was part of the reason why he was the man he was today. He hadn't been able to grieve his parents properly. Rather, he'd stuffed his own emotions deep within his heart in order to survive and care for his younger siblings. They'd had enough grief to deal with without seeing his.

He didn't hate his life, but there were times he wondered where he might have gone if not for the way life had turned out for him. But he was a man of faith, and for whatever reason, God had settled him here. Who was he to argue?

Ruby had filled in many details of Aidan's situation when Sharpe had mentioned that Emma and Aidan would be coming to the farm. Sharpe now knew Emma was Aidan's older sister and that she'd recently become guardian over the boy.

Clearly, the lad needed a strong male role model, which was the main reason Sharpe had offered to help—not that he would ever have taken Emma's money under any circumstances. It wasn't her fault Aidan had ruined his pumpkins, and she had enough on her plate with all the sudden life changes she was experiencing.

As he'd told Emma, Aidan was the spitting image of a nine-year-old Sharpe, thinking only of himself and not caring whom he hurt in the process as long as he was having fun. Aidan probably hadn't even realized he was damaging someone's livelihood when he'd smashed the pumpkins on the flatbed truck.

"What do you want us to do?" Emma asked, breaking into Sharpe's thoughts.

He handed her a pair of work gloves and gestured toward the orange-dotted fields.

"As you can see, I've got two large fields of pumpkins, as well as some gourds, butternuts and acorn squash. The field on the left is for those families who want the whole experience. We bring them out on our hayrack, and they get to wander through the field and choose their own pumpkins."

"That sounds fun."

"Many people think it is."

She tilted her head up at him, her auburn eyebrows scrunching in the most adorable way. "And for the others?"

"We do the pumpkin picking for them out of the right field, bringing them back to display for sale around the gift shop. And at various functions like the Harvest Festival," he added, then pressed his lips, wishing he hadn't said that last part. No sense in rubbing it in.

"So you want us to pick the pumpkins from the right field? Where are we going to put them, though?"

"Actually, no. That's for another day. We've got a ton of customers coming by starting next weekend, so we need to get the left field ready for them."

"I thought you said they pick their own pumpkins."

"Oh, they do. But it wouldn't be nearly as fun for them if they had to break off the prickly vines first. That's our job today."

"I see," she said, although clearly she didn't.

"Aidan, it's time to get to work," Sharpe called to the boy, who groaned and slumped his shoulders. Sharpe was glad Aidan enjoyed spending time with the dog, but the boy had a lesson to learn.

With that thought in mind, he removed a pair of safety glasses and a curved knife from his saddlebag, unsheathing it so they could see its usefulness.

Emma's gaze widened almost to the size of the pumpkins in the field. Sharpe could tell she was concerned that he was offering Aidan a dangerous gardening tool, at least right off the bat. Who knew what her brother would decide to do with it?

Aidan's eyes, on the other hand, sparkled with interest.

"I thought he'd be digging in the dirt," Emma admitted, eyeing the curved blade. "With a shovel or something."

"Oh, he'll get plenty dirty." Sharpe chuckled.

"Yes, but—"

Sharpe held up a palm to stop her flow of words. This was never going to work if she questioned his every decision.

"Are all of these pumpkins ripe and ready to go?" Emma asked.

"Great question. We're looking for the dark orange ones. Give them a thump. If they sound hollow, they're ready to go. The stems will be dark green, as well."

With his own blade, Sharpe selected a large pumpkin and then leaned down and proceeded to show Aidan what he meant for the boy to do, swiping to remove nearby vines and then making a clean cut on the stem.

Surprisingly, Aidan was enthralled and carefully watched Sharpe's demonstration.

"You think you can do this on your own?" Sharpe asked Aidan.

"Yes, sir," Aidan answered.

Smiling, Sharpe lifted his black cowboy hat and scrubbed his fingers through his hair. "It's just Sharpe, okay, buddy? *Sir* is my father." Sharpe held out his right hand to the boy, and Emma watched as her brother squared his lanky shoulders and stood an inch taller.

"Okay, *Sharpe*." Aidan offered his own grin and shook Sharpe's hand. The man's eyes widened in surprise.

Sharpe was impressed at the strength of the boy's handshake and gave him a crisp nod of appreciation.

"Before you start, you'll need to put on safety glasses," Sharpe said, handing Aidan what looked like something a chemist would wear while performing experiments.

He half expected Aidan to balk at the idea, especially because he didn't have a pair for Emma, but the young man put them on and then made a face at his sister. "Look, Emma. I'm a geek, just like you when you wear your computer glasses."

"Hey, now," Sharpe said, but before he

could continue with the reprimand, Emma laughed heartily until her eyes watered. Sharpe lifted an eyebrow in question.

"Considering Aidan and I have only recently met, my little brother nailed it," she explained. "Happily, I don't have to wear *safety* glasses to see my computer, though," she said, wiping her eyes with her thumb. "But I did enjoy science in high school, geeky glasses and all."

He didn't know why that surprised him. Everything he knew about Emma spoke to her being a smart woman. But he wouldn't have guessed she'd excelled in science. He was just now starting to realize how little he knew about the fascinating Emma Fitzpatrick.

Sharpe handed Aidan and Emma each a curved blade and led them farther into the field. "Since these are the ones folks are going to pick on their own, we'll just leave each pumpkin where we cut them. It also helps if you cover them in the dry rye a bit, so they look more natural."

Sharpe stared at Emma for a moment. She had the oddest expression on her face, although he had no idea what she was thinking. Abruptly, he turned his attention back to Aidan. "Let's see what you can do."

Aidan nodded and turned to his first large pumpkin, carefully chopping back the vines before cutting the stem with an expression of sheer delight on his face. Sharpe patted him on the back and gestured toward the next pumpkin, watching Aidan closely as he cut his way through the next few.

"Boys and their toys," Emma muttered, clearly not completely comfortable with the situation. With a huff, she leaned down and started chopping the vines of the pumpkin nearest her.

"Don't worry," Sharpe assured her. "Aidan will enjoy the physical labor, not to mention learning a lesson for the future. Look at him. He's a natural. It appears to me as if your brother may have an artistic streak running through him. Or maybe he was meant to be a pumpkin farmer."

She scoffed. "Well, he certainly wasn't born and bred to do that. And I wouldn't have guessed him to be an artist, either, though admittedly I don't know him that well yet. Mostly he just plays video games." She glanced up at Sharpe, and their eyes met and held. "Then again, I also wouldn't have put a dangerous knife into his hands."

Sharpe laughed. "He's nine. I was cutting down trees with a chain saw when I was his age and monkeying up other trees to trim the branches."

She actually blanched at the thought. "Your upbringing was a great deal different than Aidan's. I suppose a kid Aidan's age might want to climb trees, but…" She gulped a breath of air. "You aren't going to give him a chain saw, are you?"

His lips twitched, but he held back a smile. "Come on, Emma. You've got to give the kid some space to grow. Isn't he mowing your grandmother's lawn for you?"

She shook her head and grabbed for the vines of the next pumpkin.

It frankly would never have occurred to her to ask Aidan to mow the lawn, not that he wouldn't be able to do it if she had. He was tall enough and strong enough, she supposed.

"There you go, then," Sharpe said, sounding a little smug. "He should be. Get him outside and take advantage of all he can do to help. Boys are like puppies. You have to wear them out every day, use up all their energy so they don't get into trouble."

She narrowed her gaze on him, though at her height she had to look way, way up to do so. "Why are you being so nice to us?"

He clutched his chest over his heart dramatically. "You wound me."

"That came out wrong," she said, her cheeks turning the color of a ripe tomato.

He leaned down to swipe at another pumpkin, giving her a chance to regain her composure.

"It's just that you have to admit it would have been so much easier for you to take my money and call it good. Instead, you offered to spend time with my brother, even after he heartlessly destroyed your poor pumpkins."

"Honestly?" He shrugged. "I guess I see a lot of myself in Aidan. I got into a fair bit of trouble of my own when I was his age. I just thought I could help him, show him what it means to be responsible. Being a kid is tougher now than it was in my day, and I feel for his circumstances."

"Well, that's very nice of you. Thank you. I just pray your kindness won't backfire on you. Aidan may remind you of yourself at that age, but I honestly have no idea how difficult my brother might be if he gets it into his head to cause more trouble."

"He's doing okay right now," Sharpe observed, gesturing toward Aidan, who was carefully carving a stem from a pumpkin and then couching it in the dead rye, Baloo barking at his side.

"That's because you gave him something to do that is holding his interest—at least for the moment. What boy wouldn't like playing with a knife? But what if you'd asked him to clean the barn?"

Sharpe stared at her but didn't speak.

"I believe you can handle Aidan if anyone can," Emma said when Sharpe remained silent. She propped her hands on her hips and captured his gaze with hers. "He already appears to respect you, and it was you who broke up that fight between the boys last week. It's just that—I'm not making excuses for him, or for me, for that matter—Aidan didn't grow up in the best of circumstances."

"I'm sorry to hear that," he said in a low monotone. He wished his voice sounded more empathetic, because he really was feeling that way toward Emma and her brother. He just didn't know how to show it. And he knew it didn't sound in his voice, either. "As I mentioned earlier, my own father passed away when I was a teenager, so I know how hard it can be on a boy not to have a strong male role model in his life."

He caught a flash of anger in Emma's eyes before she covered it and bent down to swing her curved knife across a chunk of vines. "My parents weren't *any* kind of role models. Ever. I may be the worst guardian ever, but I will do my very best for Aidan, and that's more than my parents ever did."

He noted the ice in her tone and the way she suddenly clammed up, her teeth clenched so tight he could see the pounding of her pulse in the corner of her jaw. He didn't have the slightest idea what to say to her, not with the glowering expression on her face. He had the feeling that whatever words he used would be the wrong ones.

Suddenly, though, her face softened.

"I don't know if you're aware, but I didn't even know Aidan existed until two weeks ago, as hard as that is to believe. I was completely estranged from my parents. I never called them or reached out to them in any way, and they, in turn, kept Aidan a secret from me. He didn't know he had a big sister, either. They never talked to him about me."

"I can't even imagine what that was like."

"As difficult as it may be, I'm his guardian now. I'll do whatever I have to in order to do right by him. I took family leave and have a bunch of personal time saved up, and I can do some of my work remotely, so we're going to stay at Nan's until the beginning of December while I figure out what we're going to do."

"I admire your strength." He, more than most, knew what it felt like to have to step up to the plate in an emergency. To be handed his life choices—or lack of them—on a platter and be told to dig in.

Her gaze widened on him, and she nodded before she blew out a breath. "I just wish I knew how to reach him. I don't know anything about nine-year-old boys. I understand he's going through a tough time. But when he starts getting into fights to blow off steam, I don't know what to do."

Sharpe shoved his hands into the front pockets of his jeans and pushed the toe of his boot into the grass, pressing his lips together. He wished he had something useful to say, but he didn't, so he remained silent.

She huffed out a sigh. "Speaking of which, I'd best go check up on Aidan. I don't want him accidentally carving into the pumpkins instead of trimming stems and vines."

Sharpe had kept half an eye on the boy as he'd worked, but Aidan had moved to the middle of the field, and he couldn't tell exactly what the boy was doing to each pumpkin.

He really felt for Emma. As difficult as his situation had been when his parents had died, at least he'd known his siblings and what they needed to survive. It took courage to suddenly step in as a guardian when she hadn't even known she had a brother.

And for some reason, upon which he still couldn't put his finger, he wanted to help Emma.

Maybe it was a God thing.

Or maybe he was just losing his good sense.

Chapter Three

Emma made her way over to where Aidan was in the pumpkin patch and was happy to see there were a number of well-trimmed pumpkins around him. He'd followed Sharpe's directions exactly—well, almost exactly. Her breath left her lungs when she saw what her brother had done to the pumpkin he was currently carving.

Aidan had carved around the top and taken one glove off so he could scoop out the inside goo with his hand. He'd then carved something into the pumpkin, although as Sharpe and Emma had approached him, he'd turned the pumpkin around so they couldn't see what he'd done.

Whatever he'd done, he was grinning about it. He stood and dropped the knife, pulling his safety glasses down around his neck and under his chin. "Do you want to see what I've done?"

She could *see* what he'd done—exactly what he wasn't supposed to do. But he was so excited about it, especially when he turned the pumpkin around and displayed a bright, grinning face with rainbow-shaped eyes and a huge grin with missing teeth.

"What do you think?" he asked excitedly, a bounce in his step.

What did she *think*? At this rate, Aidan was going to be here all summer trying to make up for his mistakes and to pay Sharpe back for all the money he was losing every time Aidan trashed some of his property.

Sharpe tipped off his hat and gave a low murmur.

"Well, now," he started, and Emma cringed as she waited for his reaction. He took a good look at Aidan's handiwork, pausing a moment before continuing. "I gotta say…that's absolutely amazing work. The best jack-o'-lantern I've seen in a while."

Her eyes widened on the cowboy, who, despite his kind words, was frowning.

What had he just said?

Wasn't he angry with Aidan for carving up one of his pumpkins? At least it was only *one* pumpkin this time, but that wasn't really the point, was it?

"You've got an artistic eye there, buddy," Sharpe said, tipping up the pumpkin with the toe of his boot so he could better observe it. He scratched his scruffy chin. "I like how he's grinning right up at you as if he has a secret. Not many people could do what you've done here, especially with only the one knife. I think some of my customers would really be interested in purchasing an already-carved jack-o'-lantern like this."

"Really?" Aidan was obviously pleased with Sharpe's praise, despite the fact that the man hadn't stopped frowning as he'd said it.

Sharpe didn't appear to be the kind of man to say something he didn't mean just to make someone feel better, even a kid. Emma took another look at Aidan's creation, this time appraising it more closely.

It did look like something professionally carved rather than the random cutting of a nine-year-old. Guilt plunged through her as she realized she wouldn't have given her brother the same opportunity to explain himself as Sharpe had just done, much less tried to understand what he was doing.

Still. These pumpkins belonged to Sharpe, and the cowboy had made it clear exactly how he'd wanted them trimmed. Aidan hadn't followed directions on this last pumpkin, and it hadn't been his decision to make.

"I made it special," Aidan bragged, his chest puffing out as he pushed his red curls off his forehead. "For Nan. She loves to decorate for autumn."

Emma's eyes filled with proud tears. She'd been silently struggling with what appeared to be Aidan's constant selfish behavior, so for him to think of Nan was really something. And Emma had had no idea Aidan was so artistic.

That said, the pumpkin in question didn't belong to him. It wasn't his place to go carving it out to his heart's content, however sweet the thought behind it. And it was Emma's job to make sure he understood his error. But how could she do that without hurting his feelings?

This being-a-guardian thing was hard.

While she was still struggling for the words, Aidan was digging into the front pocket of his jeans. Then he withdrew a crumpled wad of cash.

Pride swelled in Emma's chest as she realized he intended to pay for the pumpkin out of his own allowance. She definitely hadn't given him enough credit. Emma held her breath as Aidan straightened out the bills one by one. She suspected it was important that Aidan pay for what he'd created, and she hoped Sharpe realized it, too. It would take the wind out of the boy's sails if Sharpe just tried to give it to him.

"How much does one of these pumpkins cost?" Aidan asked Sharpe, holding the bills tight in his fist.

Sharpe's eyebrows rose, and he took a moment before answering, his gaze on the money in the young man's hand. Emma suspected he was trying to make an educated guess as to how much Aidan was clutching.

"These heavy ones here are called fatsos, and they're usually twelve dollars apiece, but I'll tell you what. Since you did such excellent work today, I'll give it to you for ten."

Aidan's grin widened as he peeled off two five-dollar bills and pressed them against his thigh with the palm of his free hand to flatten them out before handing them to Sharpe.

"You can take it back with you today," Sharpe said with a brisk nod, folding the bills and shoving them in his pocket. "Once we get back to the barn, I'll run out with my truck and pick it up. Trying to ride a horse with a big ol' pumpkin would be a bit of a challenge."

"We don't want to be a bother," Emma insisted. "We can come back another time to pick it up."

Sharpe shook his head. "No problem." His tone brooked no argument.

He was the strangest combination of tough and tender Emma had ever seen, and she honestly didn't know what to make of the man.

"Thank you," she said, instinctively knowing arguing with him would get her nowhere. Besides, the truth was, in a way, he intimidated her. "So what time should we come over next weekend?"

His gaze caught and held hers, and again she was struck by how deeply blue his eyes were in contrast to his dark hair.

"For?"

"Surely Aidan didn't do enough work

today to cover all the losses from the day of the Harvest Festival."

Aidan's face went red, and he toed the grass with his boot. Emma hadn't meant to embarrass him, but he had caused a good deal of trouble, and it was important that he pay Sharpe back for all the damages he'd done.

"I think he's already done plenty," Sharpe said, pressing a hand to Aidan's shoulder. "He worked hard today—definitely hard enough to cover the number of pumpkins he trampled the other day. However, I do have a question for you, Aidan."

Sharpe waited until Aidan looked up and met his eyes before continuing.

"I was very impressed by your work today. I was watching you carefully. You didn't even take a break, did you?"

"No, sir. I— It was fun," Aidan stammered.

"Well, as you can see, I have a whole other pumpkin patch to farm, and I'd appreciate it if you could come over next Saturday and trim pumpkins. These are the ones we'll be hauling back to the gift shop. I know it's all work and not exactly *fun*, but I'll pay you for your time and effort. That is, if your sister agrees it would be something worthwhile for you. I may even have regular work for you to do throughout the rest of the season, at least while you're in Whispering Pines, yeah?"

Aidan's blue eyes lit up, sparkling like the sunshine as he nodded voraciously. His Saturdays had suddenly become a lot more interesting.

Emma wondered if her little brother had even caught the part where Sharpe had reminded him how hard he'd have to work and that the jobs he would be given might not always be fun. But giving him something productive to do while they were still in town was going to be a lifesaver for Emma.

She'd been wondering how exactly she was going to follow Sharpe's advice and get Aidan outdoors and away from constant screen time, like perhaps mowing Nan's small lawn and doing some landscaping at her house. It wasn't so much that Emma minded Aidan playing video games if it got him out of his own head—because she knew better than anyone the trauma he'd been through—but fresh air and sunshine had to be good for him. And if he got to work with Sharpe, the man could be a good mentor to him. Who knew what kinds of skills Aidan would learn working with Sharpe? Not only that, but Emma had a ton of paperwork to go through in order to fulfill her parents' very confusing estate and Aidan's guardianship with the court.

"Please, Emma," Aidan begged, clasping his hands together under his chin. She'd rarely seen him so enthusiastic and wondered if Sharpe knew what he was getting himself into.

Well, Sharpe had been the one who'd said he understood how a preteen boy's mind worked.

"Please say yes." Aidan was so excited by the prospect his cheeks turned the color of his hair.

Emma met Sharpe's gaze. If she wasn't mistaken, there was a hint of a smile hovering on the man's lips. Maybe he really did know how important this was to the boy. "If it's okay with Sharpe, it's okay with me. But there are going to be rules, all right?"

"Oh, Emma," Aidan huffed, scowling as his face reddened even more. She'd thought he'd throw his arms around her in delight, and instead he was being surly with her.

"Exactly. You just proved my point," she said, her arms akimbo and her chin tilted down at her little brother. "There will be no attitude. You *will* respect Sharpe and do whatever he tells you, without giving him guff. Understand?"

Aidan sighed and rolled his eyes.

"Is that a yes?"

"Yes," Aidan said, his voice high and squeaky. "I'll do whatever Sharpe says." The boy's expression changed from sullen when he was looking at Emma to near-on hero worship when his gaze turned to Sharpe. "How much are you going to pay me?"

"Aidan," Emma snapped, her own cheeks flushing with heat. She supposed it was a legitimate question, but the way the young man had asked mortified her. As if Sharpe owed the boy anything. Not surprisingly, her younger brother hadn't learned any kind of manners from their parents.

"How does ten dollars an hour sound, with bonuses when I notice you're working especially hard? Saturday afternoons for as long as you're in town. Sound like a plan?"

Emma thought it was more than fair, but for some reason, Aidan hesitated for a moment, not immediately answering. How many troublemaking nine-year-old boys would get an opportunity handed to him the way Sharpe had just done?

"Money for new video games," Emma whispered to him, nudging Aidan toward Sharpe, wondering why he was hesitating.

"Yeah, okay," he said at last.

Sharpe put out his hand, and Aidan shook it, once again straightening as he did so. Sharpe was treating him like a young man and not a little boy, and Aidan was responding positively to that, information Emma tucked into the back of her mind to mull over later.

As for herself, she was grateful beyond words for what Sharpe was doing. She didn't know how she would ever be able to thank Sharpe enough for taking Aidan on as a mentee. But she did have to wonder why. Granted, Aidan was young, strong and athletic, and if he cooperated, Sharpe could possibly get some good work out of him. He'd been carrying around those thirty-to fifty-pound fatso pumpkins as if they weighed nothing, and as Sharpe had said, young boys had plenty of energy to burn.

But somehow, Emma felt it was more than that.

She couldn't help but ponder what was really driving Sharpe's kindness toward her brother—and she wouldn't stop until she found out the truth.

Sharpe was already out in the Winslow's Woodlands parking lot the following Saturday afternoon, Baloo at his heels as he directed traffic so as many cars could park within the small dirt-covered lot as possible. Parking was free, and they kept the fee for entrance to the farm low so everyone could enjoy it. Depending on the time of year, they made their money selling pumpkins, Christmas trees, evergreen shrubs and landscaping materials, as well as experiences including hayrack or sleigh rides, a lake for skating in the winter and fishing in the summer, a farm-animal petting zoo, pumpkin picking and cutting down Christmas trees. His sister Felicity ran a successful gift shop that offered both general Colorado merchandise as well as stuff that was unique to Winslow's Woodlands.

Autumn through Christmas was their busiest time of the year, and the parking lot was packed. While he was busy, Sharpe had his eyes peeled for Emma's black sedan. When he finally saw her pull into the lot, his heart leaped into his throat, an experience he wasn't used to. He tried to tell himself it was because God was using him to have a positive influence on Aidan, but while that was true, he couldn't fool himself that Aidan was the *only* reason he was excited they were here.

Emma pulled up next to Sharpe and rolled down her window. "Where should we park?"

Sharpe pointed to a spot right next to the entrance, which he'd blocked with an orange cone. "I saved it for you," he said with a grin.

"You didn't have to do that," she protested.

"I've seen the kind of shoes you wear," he teased. "Until you invest in a pair of practical boots, you'll get the best parking space I've got."

"You do realize you're persuading me to do the exact opposite of what you want me to do," she said. "Why would I give up my front-row parking in exchange for a pair of ugly boots and a longer walk to the entrance?"

"Hey," he protested. "Cowboy boots don't have to be ugly. And at the very least, you'll need a good pair of snow boots or hiking boots pretty soon. Snow comes early to the mountains. Boots are a given up here."

"Do you need me to stay?" she asked. "I

have a myriad of things I need to do back at Nan's, but if you need me to stay for Aidan, I'm happy to do that."

"I can handle Aidan, but I have something I'd like to show you. It won't take long."

Sharpe actually felt eager. He didn't know what it was about Emma that made him *feel* so strongly when she was around him, but there it was. He probably ought to be running in the other direction, but she wasn't going to be in town long, so his heart was safe.

"Sure, if you want." She exited her car with a grin that sent a frisson of awareness down his spine and pointed at her boot-clad feet. They weren't cowboy boots, but the heel was a couple of inches smaller than what he'd seen her wear up until this point, maybe two inches instead of four and square-heeled rather than spiked.

"Better," he said, tipping his hat, "but I'm not giving up until you learn the real definition of the word *practical*."

"Are we going to use a knife and cut pumpkins again today?" Aidan asked, his voice cracking with excitement. He came around the back of the car to join the adults, then crouched down to pet Baloo, who welcomed him with excited tail wagging.

"I don't really know what to expect, and neither should you," she reminded him gently.

Sharpe remained silent, shoving his hands into the front pockets of his jeans and rocking back on his heels.

"But I did such a good job last week."

Sharpe met Emma's gaze, and she sighed. Her brother was back to whining again. Sharpe suspected she was going to have to learn to deal with that. Aidan had just suffered through the loss of his parents. A little whining was to be expected.

"You did," she agreed. "I was really proud of you. And Sharpe obviously recognized how well you did, as well, or he wouldn't have asked you to work with him."

"Work *with* me, not *for* me," Sharpe emphasized.

"Like a mentor."

"Exactly."

Emma pressed a palm to her heart. "I'm grateful."

Sharpe shrugged, feeling oddly self-conscious, an emotion he wasn't used to feeling. "We're going to work on bringing some pumpkins and gourds back to the gift shop later this afternoon, but first I have another job for you—one you may not like as much."

"If you want to earn the money he's offering, you have to do whatever he asks of you," she reminded Aidan.

"Whatever," he said.

Sharpe understood more than most why the boy acted the way he did, but he could see by the expression on Emma's face she had no idea how to break through this barrier. Hopefully he'd be able to help a little in that regard, teach Aidan how to be responsible and respectful the way a man ought to be. At the moment, the boy was more interested in Baloo, who was leading him on a merry chase around the parked cars.

"I have something special I want to show you two," Sharpe said loud enough for Aidan to hear, as well, and hopefully pique his interest. "Follow me."

He turned and walked off toward the entrance, glancing back only once to see if they were following.

After a minute or so, he could tell Emma was having a bit of trouble navigating the bumpy gravel terrain. He heard her small squeaks of distress, even though he could tell she was trying not to let him know she was having any difficulty. Sharpe stopped and held out his hand to her, enveloping her small, soft hand in his large, calloused one.

"It can get a bit tricky walking these gravel trails," he said with an understanding smile. "Especially in…" He nodded toward her boots.

"Right," she agreed through gritted teeth. "As if I'm the only city girl who has ever visited Winslow's Woodlands wearing the wrong shoes. Trucks drive across most of these trails. Surely I should be able to manage to walk them without this much trouble."

"Lots of people visit from the city. We try to keep the gravel paths even, and we've even talked about putting in concrete, but at the end of the day, Winslow's Woodlands is a farm, and visitors come to experience the whole farm experience, so we decided to stay with the gravel."

"Makes sense," she agreed. "You're giving your visitors the whole package. From what I've seen so far, it's very quaint. I would never have thought about going to a farm to pick out my own pumpkin. I didn't even know it was a thing. I've always bought them from the local grocery store."

"Now, see what you've been missing? And just wait until you see what I've got to show you today."

"Call me intrigued," she said, tapping her chin with her well-manicured index finger that Sharpe instantly compared with his own dirt-under-the-nail fingernails. Once again feeling self-conscious, he dropped his hand from hers.

She wobbled again, and he slowed down, taking her elbow to help keep her upright.

"Better than pumpkins?" she asked.

He chuckled. "Depends on who you talk to. But, yeah. I'm thinking for you, it'll be better than pumpkins. Let's head for the barn."

When they walked into the shade of the barn from the sunshine, Sharpe waited a moment for their eyes to adjust, then grabbed a shovel and rake, holding them out to Aidan with a grin. "The stalls need cleaning out before we go cut pumpkins. Rake the dirty straw into the front corner of the stalls, and then use the shovel to scoop it into the wheelbarrow. When it's full, I'll show you where to dump it."

"Seriously?" Aidan said, immediately balking and wrinkling his nose.

"Do I look serious?" Sharpe raised a brow, though it was all he could do not to crack a smile.

Man and boy squared off for a moment, their eyes locked, until finally Aidan looked away, staring angrily at the ground.

"I told you last Saturday that you may not like every job I give you," Sharpe reminded him. "But as chores go, cleaning the stalls isn't all that bad. Feel free to groom Diamond if you want and spend some time bonding with her. The brushes are on the wall. Get to know her a little bit better before we ride out to the pumpkin patch later this afternoon."

Aidan's lips twitched for a moment, as if he was deciding what to say, but in the end, he just said, "Okay. Where do I start?"

Sharpe grabbed the wheelbarrow and pushed it down to the end of the line of stalls. "Start with this one and work your way forward. Once you're finished, you can play with Blue—*Baloo*—for a while if you want until your sister and I are done here. There's a basket of toys just outside the barn door. Baloo especially likes to play tug-of-war and fetch."

"Oh! Fetch will be a good one," Emma said, nodding. "Aidan is the pitcher on his baseball team." It was one of the few facts she'd been able to glean from her mostly closemouthed brother, and she wanted him to know she was proud of him for whatever extracurricular activities he chose.

"Are you any good?" Sharpe asked.

"Best in my league," Aidan said.

"Well, then," Sharpe said. "There you go. Tossing a ball for Baloo will be good for your arm. You can go out in back of the barn and throw as hard as you want. There's a huge empty field there."

"Practice makes perfect," Emma added.

Aidan rolled his eyes and entered the first stall, noisily clanking the door closed behind him. Sharpe heard the horse startle and chuff, so he leaned his forearm over the top of the stall door so Aidan could see him. "Easy there, cowboy. Sudden noises startle animals."

Sharpe watched as Aidan put earbuds into his ears and turned on music from his phone before he took the rake and scooped the dirty straw into the front corner of the stall. Sharpe almost told him to lose the music so he'd be more aware of the animals and his surroundings, but in the end, he just let it go, picking his battles with the boy and suspecting there would be many more to come.

He turned to Emma, anxious to show her what he'd brought her into the barn for. He waved her into a stall on the opposite side of where Aidan was working.

"Come see," he whispered, holding the stall door open for her. When she'd entered, he moved to the back corner of the stall and stooped to scoop up two tiny bundles of fur into his palm. "Mama Cat had six little ones last week," he explained, handing her one of the kittens.

Emma made a mewling sound that was rather like the orange tabby kitten she immediately snuggled under her chin. "He's adorable."

"I thought you'd like him and his brothers and sisters. As a responsible animal shelter, we make sure all of our cats and dogs are spayed and neutered, but this mama barn cat came in already pregnant, and my sisters with their soft hearts just couldn't turn her away."

"Your *sisters* with their soft hearts," she repeated, her eyes twinkling as she gestured toward the kitten he held curled in his palm. "Right."

"What? You're shocked that a guy like me would enjoy a litter of newborn kittens?"

"No," she exclaimed, pressing a hand to her flaming cheek. "That's not what I meant at all. But you have to admit, you look a little incongruous."

"Okay, I'll admit it. I was the one who found them," he explained. "I ride my horse most mornings to clear my mind and pray." It was one of the only times in his life when he felt a sense of freedom, though he didn't say that aloud. "Anyway, one morning this very pregnant but scroungy mama barn cat crossed my path. She's not feral. Maybe she got lost or her owner dumped her when they discovered she was pregnant. She welcomed this nice warm stall with fresh, clean straw."

Emma inhaled deeply. "Oddly enough, I can understand why."

Their eyes met, and he had the feeling she really did understand him, even the words he wasn't saying. It should have given him comfort, but instead it made his insides flutter.

"As I said, no one in my family objected to a litter of kittens, but they'll be expecting me to find them all good homes. I don't suppose you want to adopt one. Or two. Two is always better than one, where kittens are concerned."

He gave her his best grin, even as she shook her head.

"As much as I adore kittens, I'm afraid that's not an option," she said, giving the orange tabby one last cuddle before placing him back with his mama. "Where I live right now, there isn't even room for a kid, much less a kitten. I'm still not sure how this is going to work out."

The smile the kittens had put on her face moments before immediately disappeared, and stress lines creased her forehead. Sharpe half wished he hadn't brought it up at all, even though he'd kinda, sorta been joking about taking a kitten. While he really was the one responsible for adopting them out, he hadn't expected her to take one.

And now he'd reminded her of the trouble that lay ahead of her, and it gutted him, because he was a man who liked to solve problems. And he could do nothing for Emma.

"I'm sorry," he apologized, and her gaze widened.

"For what? It's not your fault I chose to live in a tiny apartment complex."

He shrugged. "Well, no, but I shouldn't have bothered you with the kittens. I know you have a lot on your plate right now. I wasn't thinking."

She reached out and touched his forearm, her gaze warm. "You weren't wrong. I enjoyed the kittens. But, yes, I have a lot to think about right now."

"Do you want to talk about it?" he offered, half hoping she'd decline. He wasn't much of a conversationalist. But this was about her, and he wanted to be a good friend.

"I'm mostly good with all the legal stuff I've been working my way through. Signing a few documents has been the least of my worries. The harder part is going to be getting to know my brother so I can be a decent guardian for him."

"Will you be heading out to your parents' home to clean it out before you head back for California?"

She frowned, and her copper eyes darkened. Once again he balked at what he'd done. He didn't usually get personal with people, and he had no idea why he'd blurted out such a delicate question. He supposed her situation had brought to mind his own parents' deaths. He remembered the pain of having to go through their personal items and decide what to keep and what to give away. It had been the little things—his mother's unique scent lingering on her clothes and his father's favorite chessboard—that had torn him up inside. To this day, that was one of the hardest things he'd ever had to deal with.

"We grew up in an upper-middle-class suburb of Chicago," she told him. "My parents had an apartment there. And to answer your question—no, I'm not going out there. There's nothing I want to keep from that place. There's a good reason I left home when I turned eighteen and never looked back. My lawyer is setting up an estate sale for whatever my parents had in their apartment, and I'll tuck the money I make from it into a trust for Aidan's future. I really have no other use for it."

Bitterness fairly crackled from her voice as she spoke. It sounded as if she hadn't had a wonderful upbringing, and from the way her gaze hardened when she spoke of her parents, he guessed she hadn't been close to them. He was grateful for the relationship he'd had with his own parents but felt bad for Emma.

By this time, Aidan had finished mucking out the stalls and had hosed off the wheelbarrow. Sharpe could hear him outside calling to the dog to play with him.

"Come on, Baloo. Fetch!" Aidan hollered, followed by a joyfully barking dog who was happy to have a young boy to play with.

Sharpe crouched down to untangle the mess of hose Aidan had left, which looked rather like the same kind of knot his stomach was in. "So you're determined to take Aidan back to LA with you when you have everything resolved, then?"

He didn't know why that would matter one way or another to him. He'd just met this woman, yet already he felt as if they could be good friends.

She sighed. "I suppose, although like I said, I'll have to find somewhere else for us to live, because my current loft is far too small for both Aidan and me. I'll probably see if I can find something suitable online, though we may just stay in a hotel until we find something. There's a lot I still have to figure out. I'm glad I have a couple of months of paid time off just to sort out the specifics."

Emma folded her arms tightly around herself, and Sharpe thought he saw her shiver even though the barn was warm. There was a long, awkward silence as she gazed off into the distance, her stare blank and her expression miserable.

At that moment, Sharpe grabbed the sprayer and was stunned when a stream of water shot out, blasting him under the chin and soaking his shirt.

He hollered and jumped up, dropping the hose.

Emma clapped her hand over her mouth, but her eyes were dancing with amusement, and he could tell she was laughing.

At him.

But he supposed it beat the sadness that had been there previously.

"I'm so sorry," Emma said, though her words were bubbling with giggles. "I guess he didn't turn off the water when he put the hose away."

This whole situation should have annoyed him, but then again, it had broken the stiff silence that had fallen between them, and there was a lot to be said for that.

He caught her gaze and grinned. "I guess not."

Chapter Four

Emma and Sharpe had settled on visiting the veterans' shelter on the following Thursday afternoon. She wasn't sure how to dress to visit a homeless shelter, so she opted for jeans, an emerald green cotton pullover and hiking boots. She'd spent extra time selecting the shirt, wanting it to be functional, since she had no idea what she'd be doing today, and yet likewise wanting to address the niggling in her stomach to put on something nice that would catch Sharpe's eye.

Not that he'd notice her shirt. Not that she would expect him to. And not that she ought to be pursuing *any* of those thoughts or where they might be leading her. She'd be gone in a month and a half, and Sharpe and Winslow's Woodlands would be nothing more than a

pleasant memory. She acknowledged her at-
traction to the handsome cowboy and mind-
fully set it aside.

As she remembered the way he'd stepped
in and handled that fight between the boys
that first afternoon at the festival, Sharpe
struck her as the ultimate in practicality.

Whatever needed doing, he did.

Full stop.

She was of a similar nature, wanting to
reach out and help anyone who could benefit,
though she wasn't sure what she'd be able to
do to help homeless veterans. She was anxious and excited to find out more and was
glad Sharpe had invited her along.

Emma suspected this visit today had a lot
to do with Aidan, giving him a whole new
experience with how other people lived. Her
brother often complained that he had it so
bad—and she acknowledged that he did, in
a way. She knew how difficult it must have
been for him, growing up with their parents.
Even after all these years, she felt nothing
but anger toward her father and mother. Her
childhood had been spent hiding away from
her parents' anger. The constant fighting and
screaming. The emotional abuse and control

issues. It was no wonder she'd fled as soon as she was able and had cut all ties with them.

She wouldn't be surprised to find out Aidan felt the same. Had their father been as hard on him as he'd been on her, or had it been different for him because he was a boy?

Emma didn't know, and they weren't yet close enough for her to question him about that. But whatever he'd experienced growing up, he was free from that now, and though he now had to accept Emma as his guardian, she was determined to make Aidan's future better than his past.

She and Aidan were ready and waiting in the living room when Sharpe knocked on the door to Nan's house. They loaded up in his black dual-cab truck, Aidan in the back seat with Baloo, and headed for Denver, about an hour-and-a-half drive from Whispering Pines. At first, Emma made small talk, but Sharpe didn't seem to have much to say. The quieter he was, the more she prattled. She talked when she was nervous.

With effort, she closed her mouth and watched the scenery. The drive down the mountain was beautiful. It was so very different from downtown LA, and she'd never get enough of the stately lodgepole pines and the way the aspen trees' golden leaves flickered in the sunlight.

When they crested a mountaintop and she could suddenly see Denver's stunning skyline, she took in a surprised breath and turned to Sharpe. "Can you give me some idea of what to expect? What do you usually do while you're at the shelter?"

Without taking his eyes off the road, Sharpe shrugged. "Depends on the day."

Well, that was totally not helpful. She remained silent, hoping he'd elaborate on his own.

Eventually, he did.

"Today, we'll be getting there around lunchtime, and they always need people to help serve the food. Plus, it's a great way to introduce yourself to whoever's there, as it changes from day to day."

He glanced in the rearview mirror at Aidan, who was sitting in the back seat of the dual-cab pickup with Baloo's head resting on his lap. The boy's eyes were closed, and he looked as if he was sleeping.

"Hey, buddy?"

No answer.

"Is he sleeping?" Sharpe asked.

Emma chuckled.

"Earbuds," she explained, then turned around and waved to get Aidan's attention, motioning for him to remove his headphones.

Aidan popped out his right earbud. "Yeah?"

"Sharpe has something to say to you."

"What?"

"Watch the attitude," Emma reminded him. He responded with his usual scowl.

"Can you be in charge of Blue—*Baloo*—while we're at the shelter? It's an important job."

Aidan flushed in delight and smiled.

Emma wished she could get the same kind of response from her brother, but they were still trying to get to know each other and navigate the new path of Emma suddenly becoming Aidan's legal guardian. She sometimes felt it was one misstep after another on her part.

Sharpe, on the other hand, could do no wrong in Aidan's eyes.

Emma sighed inwardly, reminding herself to be grateful Sharpe was there and that he was willing to mentor Aidan during what surely must be the most difficult time in her brother's young life.

Once they were in downtown Denver, with skyscrapers on every side, Sharpe navigated the mostly one-way streets with ease and then pulled into a four-hour paid parking lot.

When they'd exited the vehicle, Sharpe grabbed a large canvas bag he explained was full of packages of hand and foot warmers that would be especially useful to the men during the upcoming winter, when Denver's weather often dropped below zero at night. Sharpe then showed Aidan how to fasten Baloo's red service dog vest around him, allowing the boy to do the honors on his own.

"Well done," Sharpe praised, making Aidan beam. "You just learned the first trick of using a service dog. The vest is very important, so people know Baloo is a working dog and not just a pet. Now, keep a good hold of his lead as we walk to the shelter," Sharpe told Aidan. "Especially while we're outside. There's a lot of crazy traffic around here, and we have to be extra careful."

That was certainly true, though it felt familiar to Emma. There was a constant stream of traffic, making crossing the street difficult.

"It's not as bad as LA," Emma remarked. "Now, *that* traffic is truly insane. I don't like to drive in it."

"I can only imagine."

"You've never been to California?"

He shook his head. She didn't know whether it was her imagination or perhaps the direct sunlight, but it looked almost as if Sharpe was gritting his teeth under his two-day growth of beard.

"I've never been anywhere," he admitted with a tight shrug, the corners of his lips curving into a frown. "The truth is, downtown Denver is as far as I've ever gotten away from Whispering Pines in my whole life."

Wow.

Sharpe really put the *country* in country boy. She'd found that she very much liked the small mountain town of Whispering Pines, despite it being so different from anything she'd ever experienced, but she couldn't imagine not wanting to see more of the world than that tiny corner. Her bucket list was full of all the places she wanted to see, in all parts of the world. She glanced back at Sharpe, wondering what was on his bucket list.

She was about to ask when Sharpe abruptly

stopped before what appeared to be an old, dirty glass storefront.

"This is it," he said, gesturing at the door.

They'd passed several men and women lounging in front of buildings or under the shade of sparse trees, people who carried their entire lives in a canvas bag or beat-up shopping cart, but that was nothing compared to what Emma saw when they passed through the glass door and into the military veterans' homeless shelter.

Men of all ages and races were spread across rows of cots set wall to wall across the front room. Some of them napped on their backs, while others curled on their sides, blankly staring forward or at a whitewashed wall. Other men huddled around each other in small groups, talking or playing cards to pass the time. To Emma's surprise, some looked freshly showered and shaved, while others looked more like she'd expected homeless men to look, with long hair and bushy beards that told stories Emma knew would break her heart to hear.

She'd known this was going to be hard, but when had that ever stopped her? She mentally squared her shoulders and turned to Sharpe.

She didn't know what she and Aidan would experience today, but she was ready for whatever came at them.

"Lead the way," she told Sharpe, resting her palm against his bicep.

Before Sharpe could respond, an enormous, boisterous man who was at least six-six and two hundred and fifty solid pounds came rushing straight at Sharpe, a big grin lining his face. He was dressed in torn jeans, a ragtag beige T-shirt and a tan boonie hat, but what Emma most noticed was his spit-polished black military boots. Just before he and Sharpe collided, they clasped opposite hands and bumped shoulders.

To Emma's pure astonishment, Sharpe's smile was at least as big as the other man's.

"Hey, old man. How ya doin'?" Sharpe asked.

"As if you have to ask. Full-on busy, as usual. Today has been as nutty as a squirrel's den just before winter hibernation. Glad you're here to help."

His gaze shifted to Emma and Aidan. Her brother stood motionless, his eyes wide as he clasped Baloo's leash tight in his left fist.

"This is Emma and her little brother,

Aidan," Sharpe said, and Emma held out her hand to the man. "Emma, this old coot is former Delta Force operator Tre'Monte Williams, though everyone around here calls him Mongoose."

"Mongoose?" she questioned aloud, her voice a high squeak. "Um…what kind of nickname is that?"

"Trust me," Sharpe said with a laugh. "Never has a nickname fit an individual so perfectly. This guy," he said, pointing his thumb toward Mongoose, "once quite literally stared down a cobra at striking distance and won bare-handed—or so the story goes. Of course, he can't tell you where or when, or he'll have to kill you afterward."

Mongoose threw back his head and let out a deep, rich laugh. He then reached his hand out to Emma and pumped her arm with so much enthusiasm she couldn't help but respond to his beaming smile and firm handshake.

"I was just about to show them around," Sharpe said, gently wrapping an arm around her shoulders in an almost possessive manner that surprised her.

She glanced up at Sharpe but couldn't read

his expression. She thought, not for the first time, that he was very good at wiping away his emotions with the expediency of an eraser on a whiteboard so they didn't show on his face.

"Come on," Sharpe said, his tone suddenly gravelly, though not unkind. "Let me show you the kitchen."

"I'm going that way," Mongoose said, holding his elbow out to Emma. "Allow me."

This time Emma thought she saw a hint of annoyance in Sharpe's face. He obviously liked and respected the man he affectionately called Mongoose, yet she was positive she could feel the tension in the air and wondered if Sharpe was regretting having offered to bring Emma and Aidan to the shelter.

Keeping up a steady stream of conversation, Mongoose accompanied them to the utilitarian kitchen and explained how meal production worked, but he didn't follow them when they moved on to tour the rest of the shelter.

Aidan remained close to Sharpe as they walked. Emma smiled encouragement at her brother when she caught his eyes. He would never admit to it, of course, but she thought he was probably a little bit overwhelmed and intimidated by everything he was seeing.

"Bathrooms and showers over there," Sharpe said as they passed a door marked Gents. "The shelter provides as much in the way of usable clothing as people donate, but it's not nearly enough. There's always a special need for heavy coats in winter. That's also why I bring along the hand and foot warmers this time of year. The men can tuck them into their gloves or boots, and it really helps keep their extremities warm during the worst of it."

Emma shivered as she imagined the homeless in winter. "I can't imagine being that cold with nowhere to go, especially with all the snow."

"It's tough. And that's where this facility and others like it come in, to give shelter to as many homeless as possible. There are never enough beds for all those who need it, and it's a continually growing need, what with soldiers suffering from PTSD and traumatic brain injuries, which, left untreated, often lead to substance abuse and/or homelessness. The men are trying to ease their pain any way they can."

He paused and shook his head, then gestured toward the door in front of them. "This is the computer room, where the vets can check their email and apply for jobs. It's one of the most critical ways to help them make new lives for themselves."

Emma glanced around the mostly empty room. There were five computer stations but only one in use. She supposed checking email or surfing social media wasn't likely at the top of many of the vets' to-do lists when finding a hot meal and a place to sleep was a daily struggle.

"There's a conference room in the back where Mongoose offers various classes to help those who are ready to get back on their feet. He brings in specialists to help the vets build their résumés and teaches them soft skills that will help them with the interview process."

"Those who are ready?" Emma queried softly, compassion swelling in her chest at the thought that many of these men probably weren't ready to be helped. She wondered how one could reach out to such men and women.

Sharpe glanced at the young vet huddled

over the computer in the far corner of the room and reached for Emma's elbow, turning her away before tipping his head down and answering her question in a low tone.

"Not every veteran is ready or able to help themselves. Until they make that crucial decision for themselves, we give them as much support as they are willing to accept. I have a friend from high school—David—who was a homeless vet for a while, and it about tore me apart. That's actually how I started volunteering here at Mongoose's shelter. I knew David slept here from time to time. When I saw how many others there were that were just like my friend, I couldn't help but want to do what I could. Remind me and I'll tell you more about David on the ride home."

Emma nodded, but in truth, she couldn't imagine the level of despondency these men and women lived with day in and day out, and she said as much.

"That's where Baloo comes in," Sharpe said, gesturing Aidan to his side. "Baloo can sometimes reach these guys when humans can't. Do you want to come with me and see how it's done?" he asked the boy.

Aidan's gaze was wide, and Emma read

fear in his blue eyes, but if Sharpe noticed, he gave no indication of it. He rested his large, gentle hand on Aidan's shoulder and didn't look back as he went through the door and into the front room.

"Come on, buddy. It's time for you and Baloo to get to work," she heard him say.

Emma watched after them as they left the computer room, wondering what she was supposed to do now. Follow Sharpe out to the main room and watch Aidan and Baloo?

Or was she supposed to find something actually useful to do? After all, she was here to volunteer, not to stand there gaping while other people helped out.

She felt more than a little awkward just standing there in the mostly empty computer room by herself. Of course she did. This whole experience was new to her. It was like taking off blinders she'd worn her whole life.

Determined to make a difference, she turned to the lone vet in the computer room.

"Hi. My name is Emma. Is there any way I can help you today?"

Sharpe knew the names of many of the men currently taking up cots at the shelter. He guided Aidan and Baloo to a small group of older vets who were huddled in a semicircle, shooting the breeze.

"Hey, guys, I'd like you to meet Aidan," he said, gesturing to the boy, who was, not surprisingly, hanging back and appearing a little shy.

"And who is this furry guy here?" The man on the cot closest to Aidan directed his question to the boy. Sharpe was acquainted with the man, whose name was Jordan. They'd met on Sharpe's previous visits to the shelter. And Jordan had likewise already met Baloo. But he didn't say so. Instead, he was trying to draw Aidan into the conversation.

"His name is Baloo," Aidan replied after a short pause. Sharpe helped him nudge the border collie closer to the vet. Aidan understood what Sharpe intended and led Baloo to the middle of the group, where he was more easily accessible to all the men. "He's a border collie, and he likes to fetch and play tug-of-war."

Before long, Aidan seemed to have lost any reticence he'd originally had as the vets asked him questions about his favorite subjects in school and what he did for fun.

"I like math and computer coding," Aidan replied, petting Baloo without even realizing he was doing so. The pup wasn't just bringing joy to the vets but was easing Aidan's anxiety without the boy even knowing he was doing so. "And I hate reading."

"I hear you," a vet nicknamed Click agreed. "Other than the ones I had to study for the army, I haven't picked up a book since the day I graduated from high school. That's cool, though, about the computer coding. You can always get a job when you know stuff like that."

"Aw, come on, now," said a corpsman vet nicknamed Doc, shaking his head. "We ought to be encouraging the boy to read. You can learn a lot from a book. Or at the very least, it can take you away from reality for a while and put you into a better place. I read constantly when I was marking time at Walter Reed hospital."

"You were in the hospital?" Aidan asked, his eyes widening.

"Yeah. Got a little banged up, and they practically had to glue me back together. It's all good now, though."

Sharpe knew it *wasn't* all good. Doc was

living on the street, and his legitimate need for medication to dull the constant pain he was in had eventually led him to using illegal drugs. But he appreciated that every one of these vets was being so kind to Aidan. In other ways, Sharpe knew young Aidan's presence was good for the vets, as well, reminding them of better days.

Spending time here volunteering at the shelter was becoming increasingly important to Sharpe, and it meant a lot to him that he was able to share it with Emma and Aidan.

As Aidan made his way around the room, sharing Baloo with some of the other men, Sharpe turned to see if Emma was watching her little brother and the dog. He was certain she'd be proud of how well Aidan was interacting with the vets.

Sharpe had expected her to follow them when he'd led Aidan out to the front room, but he'd been so caught up making sure the boy was comfortable that he hadn't noticed Emma wasn't right behind him.

Guilt struck him a low blow right in the gut. He was responsible for her well-being here, since he'd been the one to invite her.

And then he'd just walked away and left her to fend for herself?

Plus, it was almost time to help serve lunch.

He glanced around and was relieved to find her in the far corner of the room, chatting with one of the vets whose long, dark, freshly combed hair and beard were still wet from taking a shower. Emma held a coffee carafe in one hand and was filling mugs as she moved around the room, smiling and speaking with each vet in turn, making eye contact and taking time with each man.

Sharpe's heart gripped with emotion as he watched her. If she was nervous, he certainly couldn't see it. Her gaze gleamed with compassion.

"They're calling her the Coffee Lady," Mongoose said from behind him.

Sharpe jumped at the sound of his friend's deep voice.

Mongoose responded with a deep chuckle. "She's so friendly and outgoing. She just jumped on in without anyone having to guide her," he continued, his voice full of appreciation. "She saw a need and filled it. Boom."

Sharpe's mind was so full of thoughts and

his heart so filled with emotions, but he didn't have a clue what to say.

"And it definitely doesn't hurt that she's young and pretty. I've gotta say, I am enjoying the way her smile lights up the whole room at least as much as the rest of the men are," Mongoose said, scratching his beard to hide his grin.

Sharpe had been thinking the same thing, and he was glad for the vets' sake that Emma could brighten their day with her smile. Many of them probably hadn't had a beautiful woman's attention in quite some time, and Emma really knew how to make a man feel special.

But he wasn't sure he appreciated that Mongoose had noticed Emma's natural beauty. He narrowed his eyes on his friend.

Mongoose threw back his head and roared with laughter. "No worries, pal. I've already got a girlfriend."

Sharpe choked on his breath. There were so many things wrong with that statement, beginning with the fact that Emma wasn't his girlfriend. Sure, he'd have to be blind not to recognize her inward and outward beauty, but he didn't have any claim on her, and she'd probably be mortified to discover Mongoose thought there might be something between them, or that Sharpe had laid any kind of claim to her heart.

"Time to serve lunch," Mongoose said, gesturing toward the long serving tables, where waiting stainless-steel serving steamers had been set up down the line, Sterno burners lit under each of them.

Sharpe gestured to Aidan and, after visiting the washroom to oversee the boy carefully scrubbing his hands with soap, led him behind the serving tables to a steamer, commanding Baloo to lie at Aidan's feet. The dog was very well trained, and Sharpe knew he wouldn't budge until told to do so.

He fitted Aidan with gloves and took off the lid of the nearest steamer, revealing hot, freshly baked rolls. Sharpe handed the boy a pair of tongs.

"Place one roll on each man's plate," he explained. "But it's absolutely okay if they ask for two or come back for seconds. It looks as if we have plenty."

Sharpe then looked for Emma, wondering if he should snag her so the three of them could serve standing next to one another. But she was still busy with the coffee, darting back and forth from various men to the coffee maker, loading her arms with the men's thermoses, which she generously filled with hot coffee and returned to them with a smile.

It was hard not to just stand there and watch her work, but he knew he had work to do, as well. Sharpe turned his attention to his own warmer. When he lifted the lid, the smells of garlic and Italian seasoning flooded the area.

Sharpe took a serving spoon and stirred the penne pasta in a tomato-and-meat sauce. It was enough to make Sharpe's mouth water on the spot, even though he wouldn't be eating until all the vets had been served.

The delectable smell of the food immediately had the men queuing up at the far end of the serving tables, those near the front of the line with plates already in hand.

From there, things got busy as the servers added food to each vet's plate. Aidan's expression was grave and serious, his dark red eyebrows low over his eyes as he did his part to help each veteran receive a hot roll or two.

Sharpe leaned down to whisper in the boy's ear. "Relax and smile. You're doing an awesome job here."

Aidan grinned up at him, his gaze triumphant.

"That's better."

Emma was likewise smiling. She'd now taken her place behind the beverage table, still serving up hot coffee but now bottles of cold water, as well.

After a while, the line dwindled as the individual vets sat on their cots enjoying their warm meals.

"Grab yourself a plate," Mongoose said, filling his own plate as he talked.

Sharpe followed Emma and Aidan as they scooped the penne, mixed veggies and hot rolls onto their plates, amused by how much Aidan piled on his. He was definitely a growing boy, and he'd worked hard to build his big appetite today. Sharpe was amazingly proud of him, as if somehow he was personally invested in the boy.

"We're going to eat in the conference room," he said, directing them through the kitchen and computer room and into the conference room, where Mongoose had placed salt and pepper shakers, grated Parmesan cheese and a tub of butter for the rolls.

"You and those serving with you don't usually eat with the vets?" Emma asked.

"Most of the time we do," Mongoose explained. "But I thought we could take some quiet time back here to give us the opportunity to talk about what goes on here. I also want to be sure to answer any questions you may have."

"The first thing I have to say is I'm impressed by your setup," Emma said, her cheeks turning a pretty rose color. "I can see how hard you've worked to make a difference in these veterans' lives. I've talked with a lot of the men here today, and they are just so grateful for what you do for them. I don't know if they ever verbally express their thankfulness to you. I get the feeling many of these men have closed themselves off to keep from being further injured. But it was clear to me they understand what you've given up to be here with them."

"We do whatever we can here," Mongoose said, pressing his lips together until they momentarily disappeared under the curly tufts of his black beard. "I was blessed to come home from the war to a large, supportive family who helped me through my dark days. My mom and dad, two brothers and a sister, aunts, uncles and cousins all made sure I had what I needed physically, emotionally and spiritually. I honestly don't know what I would have done without them."

Sharpe's gut tightened. Though he'd never served in the military, his best friend from high school had. David had come home missing an arm. During the following years, David had suffered in ways Sharpe could only begin to imagine. He'd watched his friend deteriorate until there was hardly anything recognizable of the man he'd once known.

"It's not enough," Sharpe said, his voice tight. "Not. Even. Close."

Emma gaped at him for a moment, her eyes wide before her gaze switched to Mongoose and then back at Sharpe again.

It took him a moment to realize she thought he was criticizing Mongoose's setup here and expected him to apologize for his harsh statement.

Aidan had stopped eating, his fork hovering over his plate, clearly feeling the sudden tension in the room and probably wondering what the adults would say next.

"I'm so grateful for your service," Emma told Mongoose. "And for all those men in the other room. I know I won't ever really understand what they've been through. I'm just saying that—I feel there's so much more that could be said on their behalf. And done. I wish…" Her sentence came to an abrupt end, and she locked gazes with Sharpe.

Exactly.

Now she got it.

"What do you think, son?" Mongoose asked, addressing his question to Aidan, who still hadn't resumed eating.

"The guys are cool," Aidan said, his tone suggesting perhaps he hadn't expected to like them. "And they think Baloo is awesome. It was amazing. He knew just what to do to make them crack up."

"They like both of you," Mongoose said, patting Aidan's shoulder with pride. "You make them smile, and they don't get nearly enough of that in their lives."

Aidan's gaze dropped to his plate, and Sharpe noticed him squirm, probably half from Mongoose's praise and half from what had just been said. "Yes, sir."

He knew it wasn't easy for a nine-year-old boy to comprehend what he'd experienced today.

Sharpe swallowed his bite and pointed his fork toward Aidan. "You and Baloo have done a really good job today. We're all proud of you."

"And you," Mongoose said, gesturing toward Emma with his chin and bellowing out a laugh, "have been given a brand-new moniker. I don't know if you heard or not, but the boys are calling you the Coffee Lady."

Emma smiled and blushed. "I've been called worse."

"Your upbeat attitude is contagious. I can't even begin to tell you what a difference you've all made today. You're welcome back here whenever you can come."

"I think I can speak for all of us when I say we'd like that."

Chapter Five

"Hey, Coffee Lady," Sharpe said as he glanced over at Emma, who was sitting in the passenger seat of the truck on their way back to Whispering Pines after a full afternoon at the veterans' shelter in Denver. Her mind full of all she'd seen and experienced, she hadn't said much since they'd left the facility, and she remained silent as they entered the mountainous area on their way back to Whispering Pines.

Aidan had his earbuds in, and Emma had been quietly staring out the passenger window until Sharpe had interrupted her thoughts.

She glanced across at him.

"What?" she asked, bemused. She knew he'd said something but wasn't sure what it was.

"I was just saying that it's cool that the vets

gave you such a friendly moniker on your first day serving them." He chuckled. "I think they liked you."

"Believe me—I liked them, too. Very much." She paused and took in an audible breath. "Thank you for today. For trusting us enough to come with you."

"I know it isn't easy to see some of our nation's veterans living in those conditions. It's heartbreaking."

"It opened my eyes, for sure. Put my life and problems into perspective. And I think it was good for Aidan, as well. It gave him a wider life perspective."

"That was the plan. But I couldn't believe how well it worked. He was really good with Baloo. He's a natural dog trainer."

"He is. It was lovely to watch him."

Emma gazed at Sharpe, but he was watching the road, both hands gripping the steering wheel as he made the tight mountain turns. His Adam's apple bobbed as he swallowed.

"Do you help Mongoose often?"

Sharpe nodded. "As often as I can. Not as much as I'd like. Running the Christmas tree farm takes up the majority of my time. I've had to reconcile myself that my life is what it is."

"Why veterans, specifically? There have to be a lot of different homeless shelters in Denver, right?"

He gritted his teeth for a moment and narrowed his gaze.

"Earlier today I mentioned my friend David. We were best friends all the way through junior high and high school. Both of us were big for high schoolers and played linebacker on the football team." He paused and took an audible breath. "Hmm. He knew he wanted to join the army from the time he was just a little kid, and his intentions never once wavered."

He made a fist and pressed it into the edge of his seat.

"I remember the day during our senior year when the army recruiters set up a booth at our high school career day. David was so excited, just talking to the men. It didn't take any convincing at all. He was ready to sign on the dotted line that very day. The army recruiters even had a special deal where friends who enlisted together were guaranteed to go to boot camp together. David was completely sold on becoming a soldier and begged me to sign up with him. He was an only child of divorced parents. His mom and dad spent more time fighting than caring for David, so he felt as if he didn't have anyone who would care either way what he chose to do with his life."

"What about you? Do you think you would have enlisted with your friend if your family situation hadn't played into it?"

Sharpe shrugged and shook his head. "I don't know. Maybe. Probably. David and I did everything together. And I was a bit of a hothead back then. The thought of doing something positive to protect our country appealed to me. I really thought about it, and David put a lot of pressure on me, but in the end, I knew I had too many responsibilities at home taking care of my younger brother and sisters and working on the farm, so I couldn't in good conscience leave them to fend for themselves."

"But David enlisted. And you said he became homeless after being discharged. What happened to him?"

Sharpe's shoulders tightened, as did his grip on the side of his seat. Emma reached out and covered his hand with hers, just letting him know she was there for him. This couldn't be easy for him to talk about.

"You don't have to say anything if this is too painful," she whispered.

He glanced down at their hands, but to her surprise, he didn't move his hand away.

"David became a sniper—a great one. Good enough to be recruited into special ops. But one mission gone wrong is all it takes to change a person's life forever. In David's case, he came back home needing to be fitted for a prosthetic arm. I was just thankful to God it wasn't a body bag, but I don't think David felt that way."

Sharpe seemed miles away, lost in his thoughts, so she didn't interrupt him but squeezed his hand to let him know he wasn't alone.

"He couldn't cope. Like many soldiers who ended up in the hospital, he became dependent on fentanyl to buffer his pain, and that soon turned into using harder, illegal drugs. His longtime girlfriend, who he'd planned to marry once he was back stateside, couldn't handle his missing arm or his PTSD, so she ended things with him," Sharpe murmured softly under his breath and then turned his hand over, linking their fingers.

"Oh, my," Emma said softly, squeezing

Sharpe's hand once again. She'd never been in a legitimate long-term committed relationship, mostly because she didn't even know what one was supposed to look like, and besides, she'd been too busy building her career to date much. But she hoped she'd be the kind of person who wouldn't give up on her partner for any reason. Wasn't that what commitment was supposed to mean?

"As you know, David ended up living on the streets. Eventually, I was able to reconnect with him through Mongoose. I'm not going to say it was easy, because it wasn't, by any means, but by God's grace and with the help of Baloo's brother Axel, we got David clean, homed and on the right path."

"Where is he now?" she asked.

"He has a sheep farm not far from Whispering Pines. Just a few acres. It's not much, but he's found God's peace there, and that's all that really matters."

Emma noticed the shine in Sharpe's gaze, yet no tears fell. Even so, it struck a chord in her heart, and she wished she could put her arms around him and hold him tight, let him know everything was going to be all right.

"I'd like to meet David sometime," she said.

Sharpe chuckled, though mirth didn't quite reach his voice. "I am equally as positive he'd like to meet the Coffee Lady and hear how you got that particular moniker. Mongoose played a big part in saving David's life."

He swept in an audible breath and continued. "It would be a great experience for Aidan to meet David, as well, and Baloo always enjoys the opportunity to romp around with his brother Axel. It's fun to watch the dogs running around in the field, and we can show Aidan how border collies are used to herd sheep. It's quite a sight to see."

"I've got meetings with my lawyer set up for most of this week, but text me and we'll figure out a good time to go visit David. All of these new experiences are really awesome for Aidan."

And for me, she thought as Sharpe gave her hand a light squeeze.

And for me.

Between the beginning of October until after the New Year was always the busiest season for Winslow's Woodlands, and Aidan continued to come in on Saturday afternoons to help. The boy was surprisingly willing to do whatever Sharpe asked of him and had virtually lost his surly attitude, but today was going to be especially interesting for Aidan.

They'd be setting up the petting zoo today and would need someone to supervise, making sure the children were gentle with the animals and that none of them escaped the pen—the animals, not the children.

Sharpe was finishing his first cup of coffee of the day, leaning his hip against the kitchen counter as Baloo stretched out at his feet, when Gramps entered the room. Sharpe's gaze widened at how different his grandfather appeared.

"Well, don't you look dapper?" Sharpe commented with a chuckle. "I feel completely underdressed today. What's the occasion? Is there a wedding I forgot about?"

Usually, Gramps scuffled around in a tatty bathrobe and worn house shoes, his shoulders slumped as he carried around the morning paper. It had been that way ever since Grandma Joan had died two years ago. He'd fallen into a deep grief he couldn't seem to claw his way out of. With the family's help, Gramps had slowly been working through his grief, but it was only recently that he'd started to show any real interest in living again, getting dressed in clothes and dress shoes rather than his bathrobe and house shoes. Not too long ago, he'd returned to attending church on Sundays. Last month, he'd even started going back to his chess club on Tuesday evenings with some of his old pals.

Over the past three weeks or so, Gramps had suddenly had more of a spring in his step and the color had returned to his cheeks, and Sharpe had to wonder what had caused this sudden vault back into the living. He was grateful but was also curious.

Gramps snapped his suspenders and adjusted his bow tie with a secretive grin. He'd even shaved the scruff off his face, and Sharpe detected the tang of brisk, fruity aftershave wafting through the air.

That was *so* not Gramps.

Sharpe wished one of his sisters was here to interpret Gramps-speak for him. Now that all the girls were married, it was only Sharpe, Frost and Gramps left in the original big house, and though Sharpe could clearly see something new and unusual was affecting his grandfather, he had no idea what that could be.

It was almost as if...

"Don't tell me you have a sweetheart, Gramps," Sharpe guessed, not really expecting to be found correct. His grandfather was far too old to have a new ladylove, wasn't he?

As soon as Sharpe said the words, he wished them back, feeling as if they may have been hurtful. All the Winslows knew Grandma Joan had been the love of Gramps's life and the reason he'd had such a hard time carrying on after her death.

But to Sharpe's surprise, Gramps snorted and shook his head as if Sharpe had lost his marbles.

"You idiot," Gramps teased. "You can't see what's happening right in front of your eyes. Of course I'm pursuing a pretty woman and letting a little love into my heart—which is more than I can say for you. You should try it yourself sometime."

Sharpe's cheeks burned. He was trying to avoid his growing feelings toward a specific pretty woman, and this conversation wasn't helping.

"Why else would I be wearing this getup?" Gramps demanded. "You think I'm dressing up just for the fun of it?"

He slicked back his shock of white hair—thick and full, which Sharpe hoped was something he would inherit in his old age. Gramps's quivering hands returned to his bow tie, trying to straighten it, but he ended up making it even more crooked.

"Here, Gramps. Let me." Sharpe reached out and straightened the blue polka-dot tie that popped against his light blue dress shirt and navy suit jacket. "Hang on one sec, okay?"

Sharpe dashed into the mudroom with Baloo at his heels, grabbing a pair of stem clippers off the shelf. The mudroom had several rosebushes in pots lining the room, which Sharpe kept growing year-round, and he carefully eyed each plant, looking for the perfect bloom to complete Gramps's wardrobe.

When he found it—a soft pink Eden rose—he clipped it close to the bloom with just enough stem to be able to tuck through the buttonhole of Gramps's dark navy suit coat.

"Here you go," he said as he reentered the kitchen and added the rose to Gramps's blazer. "A final touch. Now you're ready to knock her dead."

Sharpe hadn't seen Gramps smile that big in—well, forever.

"So, who is this mysterious woman who is blessed to be the object of your affection?" Sharpe asked, feeling suddenly underdressed in his jeans and black T-shirt with his dusty cowboy boots, especially since Gramps had clearly buffed his own boots to a high shine to impress his lady.

"Miss Natalie Fitzpatrick," Gramps said proudly, his chest swelling like a rooster as he made his pronouncement.

At the sound of Emma's last name, Sharpe's breath lodged squarely in his throat. Emma's nan was Gramps's sweetheart?

"I see," he choked out. "So she'll be the one bringing Aidan by, then? Is, uh…her granddaughter also coming today, do you know?" he stammered as he waited for an answer. Even though she'd been quite busy managing her family and legal affairs, he'd been looking forward to seeing at least a glimpse of Emma as she dropped Aidan off for the day.

But now…

"I should think you'll see her, at least if you stop lollygagging around in the house and get out there to the parking lot. You've

got that young Fitzpatrick boy working for
you, right? He'll need a ride over here. And
Natalie hasn't had a driver's license for years
now because of the tremors her medications
give her. If you catch Emma just right, maybe
you can convince her and Aidan to stay for
the fun. Don't forget, we're having the family bonfire tonight. I've already invited Natalie, so it would be great if Emma and Aidan
stayed, as well, don't you think?"

Oh, he *thought*, all right.

Sharpe didn't know why it mattered so
much to him that Emma was coming out to
the farm, but he couldn't deny the way his
pulse ramped up at Gramps's answer. He
most definitely wanted to catch her and ask
her to stay for the excitement, both Winslow's
Woodlands' harvest fun day and the evening
with his own extended family. From what he
knew, she hadn't had many good family experiences, and there was nothing in the world
better than a Winslow bonfire on a crisp late-
October evening.

He glanced at the clock. "Guess it's about
time, then. I'd better get out there and set up
the petting zoo for the kiddos. Frost will be
busy hitching the horses to the hayrack for

the last rides of the season. We'll be switching over to the sleigh starting in November."

What he really intended to do was head straight for the parking lot so he would be sure to catch Emma before she dropped Nan and Aidan off and disappeared back to her nan's home.

"You kids have really outdone yourselves on this farm," Gramps said as he followed Sharpe out the front door. "I'm so proud of the lot of you. You've taken what Joan and I started with and added your own touch, every single one of you."

Sharpe had spent his entire life avoiding deep emotions, but even so, his heart warmed at his grandfather's encouraging words. It was times like this that he realized just how important his life's work was, even if he'd had no choice in the matter. So many times he'd wished he'd been able to make his own decisions, follow his own dreams, whatever those may have been.

But right now at this very moment, he knew he was where he was supposed to be, taking care of his family and Winslow's Woodlands. Times such as these were few and far between.

Sharpe was still smiling when he reached the barn, only to find Emma and Aidan were already there waiting for him. Aidan didn't notice when Sharpe approached, as he had his earbuds in and was dancing in his awkward nine-year-old way. The lanky, loosey-goosey movement amused Sharpe. He didn't ever remember having danced that way when he was a boy, but he was glad Aidan felt inclined to do so.

Sharpe's eyes immediately locked with Emma's, and she narrowed her gaze and tilted her head up at him, taking his measure.

"What?" Sharpe asked, taking a mental step backward and choking on the word. Her look alone stole his breath away from him.

"You."

"Me, what?"

"What's with the smile?"

"I'm not allowed to smile now?" Feeling oddly flustered, he tried to wipe the grin off his face, but despite his best efforts, his smile only widened. He was just feeling so happy that she and Aidan were here. No particular reason, or at least not anything he could put into words.

"Where's your nan?" he asked, trying to

change the subject—anything to get her attention off him.

Her gaze widened, and she gaped at him for a moment. "How'd you know I brought Nan with me today?"

"Let's just say there's a handsome old coot in his best go-to-meeting clothes and a rose tucked into his lapel waiting for her somewhere around here. If I'm not mistaken, he's looking for your nan."

Emma smothered a chuckle. "So that's why she's all gussied up today. I was wondering about that, but she wouldn't spill the beans. I asked why she was making herself up to look so nice, but she just looked at me with a twinkle in her eyes and wouldn't give me a straight answer—or any answer at all, really. She's all dressed to the nines. Perfume and everything. Wore curlers in her hair all night. Mascara. Lipstick. The works. She definitely looks her best today." She took a breath and pressed her palm to her mouth with a giggle. "So—she and your gramps have a little thing going on between them? How cute."

"I wouldn't use the word *cute* to describe Gramps. Not ever. He can be as grating as a gravel road after a thunderstorm. And anyway, I don't know for certain that they have anything *going*, per se. Only that he intends, in his own words, to *pursue* her. That sounds a little aggressive. You think your nan wants to be pursued?"

Emma clapped her hands together and held them over her heart. "Every woman wants to be pursued by the man she's interested in."

This was news to Sharpe. He didn't date much, but then again, he'd never put much effort into it. "They do?"

"Of course. We want to feel special. And I think perhaps your gramps is doing that for Nan. The moment we pulled up today, she jumped out of the car without a word to me and hobbled off as fast as her cane would carry her. She didn't even tell me in which direction she intended to go, much less who she planned to meet."

"Yeah, Gramps was the exact same way, dashing out of the house as if his tail was on fire. He told me he was meeting your nan, though. But only because I pried it out of him."

Her gaze sparkled with mirth, and they both laughed again.

"What are you laughing at?" Aidan asked, reaching down to scratch Baloo behind his ears as the dog immediately transferred his attention from Sharpe to the boy. Aidan had found the new litter of barn cats and was cuddling the orange tabby in his arms, the same one that had caught Emma's attention earlier. Baloo sniffed the tiny fur ball, but it didn't hold his interest, and Aidan was more fascinated by the dog than the cat, so he handed off the kitten to Emma.

"I'm not sure you'd think what we were laughing about was funny," Emma assured Aidan. She cuddled the tiny kitten under her chin and took a deep breath, joy evident in her expression.

The kitten made a tiny mewling cry, and she sighed with happiness. "You are the sweetest little kitty ever."

"Aidan, do you remember how to set up the petting zoo?" he asked. "We talked through it the other day. Why don't you start with the sheep and goats, okay? Then we'll get the rest of the animals into the pen."

"Awesome," Aidan exclaimed, immediately bolting off to fulfill his tasks. And the kid was smiling as he left!

"How do you do that?" she asked, shaking her head.

"Do what?"

"I can never get him excited to do *anything* the way you do, even if I throw in a reward. He's ready to leap to do your bidding with the petting zoo and smile while doing it, and you aren't even bribing him. I can't so much as get him to put his dishes in the dishwasher."

"Well, there you go, then. It appears obvious to me. Nobody, boy or girl, adult or child, likes to clean the dishes, am I right? I just asked him to go play with cute farm animals. That's a whole other thing."

"Unfortunately, I don't own any farm animals, or any animals at all, for that matter." She sighed again and tickled the orange tabby kitten under his chin. "My heart is becoming more attached every single time I hold this little one. It won't be long before I won't be able to set him down, and then I'll really be in trouble. I suppose I ought to put Julius back with his mama."

Sharpe grinned. "You've named him, have you?" he asked after Aidan was out of hearing distance. "And you're still telling me you don't want to take him with you when you go back to LA?"

"As adorable as Julius is, and yes, he most

definitely looks like an Orange Julius to me, I'm afraid where I live in LA, I…" Her sentence skidded to a sudden halt.

"Hey, you know I'm only kidding you," Sharpe assured her, reaching out to touch her shoulder and feeling how tense she was. "I'm really not trying to force a kitten on you."

She shuddered, and he desperately wished he could backtrack. He was a master at sticking his boot in his mouth and making her feel uncomfortable. Why couldn't he just keep his mouth shut?

"It's not that," she said with a sigh. "I'm just frustrated, and it has nothing to do with you. I'm getting nowhere trying to find a new apartment in LA. As I told you earlier, my current living situation isn't going to work for Aidan and me, not even for the short term. I'm all in knots about it. It wasn't anything I ever had to think about before, because my whole life revolved around me. I did what I wanted and lived where I wanted. I spent most of my time at work, so it didn't matter how small my apartment was. But at the moment, I have no idea where Aidan and I will be going when I return to work. We could maybe stay in a hotel until I can find something more permanent, but I'd hate to do that to Aidan, and I'll need to make sure wherever it is, it's in the school district that will work for him. It's one of many things I still have to figure out before we head home."

Sharpe was going to ask what kind of residence she was looking for, but Aidan charged back into the conversation, his face flushed from working and his breath coming in short heaves, leaving Sharpe's question hanging in the air.

"I've got the sheep and goats penned up," he said. "What should I do next?"

"Go ahead and halter Taco and Beans and put them in the pen, as well. Then we'll grab a llama and a few of the chickens."

"Taco and Beans?" He was happy to see Emma's eyes had regained their sparkle.

"Our two donkeys. I taught Aidan how to halter them last week. I expect you'll be calling them cute, as well."

"Can I help it if I'm a city girl? All of this is brand-new to me. And most of the farm animals really are adorable."

"You don't have to be from the city to appreciate a petting zoo, especially if you have young children. Even the locals enjoy visiting Winslow's Woodlands, and most of them grew up around farm animals."

"Aidan is certainly having the time of his life, having come from Chicago. To my knowledge, if his life was anything like my childhood, he had no pets of his own."

"Boys are meant to be raised in the country around animals."

Emma's face blanched, and Sharpe knew he'd said the wrong thing.

Again.

"Sorry," he murmured.

"No, I can see why you'd think that," she said before he could come up with a way to backtrack into her good graces. "The country has a lot to offer a boy Aidan's age. He has only good things to say about working with you, and he's even taken it upon himself to mow Nan's yard and finish all of the landscaping. I didn't even have to suggest it to him. He's just seeing what needs to be done and doing it."

"Good to hear. I told you he could be helpful."

"Yeah." She ran a hand down her face and blew out her breath. "I think you saw potential in him long before I did. It's just that— To be honest, this whole situation has completely overwhelmed me from the beginning. Not only learning that I have a brother, but that I'm now his legal guardian. Trying to figure out how that's all going to work, well, it's a lot. Much more than I anticipated. I'm technically on paid family leave, but I've had to put in some work time remotely when my team encounters anything that can't wait, and I know they're anxious to have me return. Whether I've found us permanent housing or not, I have to get back to my job. My boss is expecting me on December first, and I'm honestly starting to freak out that I won't be prepared to return."

He noticed her focus was on Aidan and how she was going to deal with having him in her life. She didn't even mention the stress of suddenly losing her parents, which had caused the whole ball to start rolling in the first place. She'd mentioned having to do mounds of legal paperwork but hadn't said anything personal where her parents were concerned. It seemed a heartbreaking thing, and he couldn't help but wonder about it. He knew how terrible he had felt when his own parents had suddenly died. His grandparents had helped step in to raise him and his siblings, but the bulk of the farmwork had gone to him.

Sharpe's gut tightened, and his throat clenched. He wasn't the greatest at reading people, but even he could see how hard she was struggling to control her emotions as she spoke of working out her circumstances. His heart ached for her. He wished he had the words to tell her how he was feeling, but nothing came.

And if he was being honest with himself, it was so much more. He wasn't ready for Emma and Aidan to leave town. He felt as if he was only just starting to get to know them at a deeper level, and though he wasn't yet ready to examine what that really meant to him, he also wasn't able to let it go.

How much worse would it be by the time they left just after the Thanksgiving holiday?

Chapter Six

Together, Emma, Aidan and Sharpe rounded up the petting-zoo animals and got them situated and ready for interaction just as a bevy of customers with excited, bright-eyed children began flooding into the farm.

Sharpe had explained how the double-gated system worked, built so the animals wouldn't bolt for freedom when humans were moving in and out of the pen. Aidan was already inside, making sure both children and animals remained safe.

To Emma's surprise, Aidan was great with not only the farm animals but the children, as well. Usually introverted, or at least as much as she'd seen him, he came out of his shell with the kids, smiling and talking as he showed a little girl who looked to be about four years old how to gently pet the goat that was nibbling at his shirtsleeve and leaving the little girl giggling up a storm.

"I can't believe the changes I'm seeing in Aidan," she said as she and Sharpe observed Aidan in action with the kids. "When I first met him, he was not only a silent, sullen child but a walking time bomb. His bad attitude leaked from every pore—not that I can blame him, knowing the kind of life he had before with my parents."

She hesitated as she fought to keep her mind from drifting back to her own childhood. That was maybe the hardest part of this whole mess. Not having to deal with all the lawyers and the paperwork. Not finding out she had a brother and that she was now his legal guardian. Not even the chaos she was experiencing as she attempted in vain to scramble to create a future for the two of them.

No—it was having to revisit her own past, remembering in crystal clear detail why she had left home the day she'd turned eighteen without once looking back. She blamed her parents for never telling her she had a brother, but it wasn't as if she'd ever reached out to them. They'd been dead to her long before they'd passed away.

"I think Snort and Oinker are Aidan's personal favorites," Sharpe said, breaking into Emma's thoughts.

"Snort and Oinker? Oh, goodness. These animals' names are just killing me here." She smothered a giggle and her eyes watered with mirth as her gaze shifted to the two enormous pigs.

"Aidan said they're potbellied pigs," Emma said. "But that can't be right, can it? I thought potbellied pigs were those cute little ones the size of small dogs that people keep as pets in their houses."

"Which is probably why these two were dumped at the end of our driveway—crates, food and all. Whoever had them to begin with intended to keep them as small pets. Clearly their prior owners didn't realize the adorable tiny piglets they'd picked up advertised as potbellied pigs—which they are—would grow. And grow. And grow."

"Are you serious? Someone dumped these pigs at the edge of your driveway? That's terrible. What if you didn't have the means to keep them? Then suddenly the responsibility of what to do with them would be all on you."

"Whoever the last owners were, they chose

well leaving the pigs at our farm, and in a way I'm grateful they didn't end up elsewhere. As it happens, we didn't already have any pigs, and Oinker and Snort are perfect additions to our petting zoo. As Aidan said, they love the attention."

"He sure likes them."

"He's not the only one. They're a big hit with kids and adults alike. They love to snort up a storm with their piggy talk, and they'll roll over and expose their tummies if they think there's any chance of getting a belly rub."

"How long have you had the petting zoo?"

"It was my sister Molly and her husband Logan's brainchild a few years ago. It started small at first and grew from there. It's kind of a weird thing with our family. Whenever one of my siblings gets married, the couple goes out of their way to add something unique to the business, something no one else has thought of to date." He grinned and bobbed his eyebrows. "But I didn't have to wait to get married to add my own idea. Well, *our* idea, really. Mine and Aidan's. I can't wait to show you later today what we came up with."

Sharpe's grin widened, and he rested his

palm on the small of her back as they watched her brother interacting with the kids and animals, Baloo never leaving his side. The dog and the boy had certainly become attached. Emma hoped it wouldn't be too much of an issue when the time came to leave. But Aidan knew Baloo was Sharpe's dog, and that was all there was to it.

Emma breathed deeply, and peace flooded her heart. She wished she could bottle up this moment and take it with her wherever she went, ready to open and inhale anytime things got too rough for her. She'd lingered today even though she really ought to go back to Nan's house to the nightmare of legal paperwork she still had to work through, a messy knot of a future with a ton of unknowns and probably several hours of marketing work before the weekend was over.

But right here, right now, breathing the refreshing mountain air mixed with the crisp but oddly not unpleasant barn scents, with Sharpe strong and steady by her side and her little brother smiling as he did when there was something about which he clearly cared, Emma felt...

Happy.

It had been a long time since she'd experienced such an emotion. For too long, she'd put her head down and plowed forward, so intent on pushing toward her career goals that she'd forgotten just to stop and live, to take a moment off just to be and enjoy God's grace with no other expectations.

Sharpe nudged her shoulder with his, nodding toward a picnic table across the way, where Gramps and Nan were sitting across from each other enjoying sandwiches, bags of chips and bottles of water. Their gazes were locked on each other, and Emma could see they were totally involved in their conversation together. Their sweet smiles warmed her heart.

"I don't even believe it. Are they holding hands across the table?" Sharpe whispered, his voice rising and cracking with amusement.

"It certainly looks that way. How—"

"Don't say it."

"What? I was only going to say—"

"*Cute.* Yeah. I know. Except, honestly—doesn't watching your nan and my gramps getting all cuddly together make you feel a little bit…?"

"Giddy?"

"I was going to say *uncomfortable*."

She slapped his shoulder with the back of her hand. "I can't believe you just said that."

He shrugged, a grin pulling at the corner of his mouth.

"They may be eighty, but they're people just like you and me," she reminded him. "Do you think you're suddenly not going to feel emotions when you hit a certain age? That your brain and your heart will just stop working?"

Again, he merely shrugged, and it occurred to her that Sharpe didn't put much stock in emotional reactions at all, or at least that she could tell. Even at his ripe old age of thirty, whatever feelings he did have he kept hidden well away.

"You're going to stay today, right?" Sharpe confirmed, his gaze catching hers with pleading in his eyes.

"I really shouldn't. I have so much to do. Not just the legal stuff but some work stuff, as well. Still, how many times in my life will I have the opportunity to experience a beautiful October afternoon at Winslow's Woodlands?"

It wasn't a hard decision to make. Not today, with the wind in her hair, the sound of the rustling aspen leaves and the scent of evergreens toying with her senses.

"Not to mention a little something special Aidan and I have to show you," he coaxed with a wink that sent a frisson of awareness through her and made her smile. "Your brother is gonna be pumped beyond belief when he gets to show you and my brother and sisters what he's built. Plus, tonight my family is having one of their infamous Winslow bonfires. You and Aidan definitely won't want to miss that."

Emma tried to envision a family bonfire and couldn't. Family time of any nature was entirely beyond her. The only family time she'd ever seen was on old TV shows, and she knew those weren't realistic. And for that reason, as well as many others, she agreed to stay into the evening.

After a couple of hours of nonstop animal interactions, Emma helped Sharpe and Aidan close down the petting zoo and put all the animals away. She found she enjoyed laying out fresh hay for Taco and Beans and even scratching the pigs on their stomachs when they rolled over on their backs begging to be petted. That never would have been on her bucket list before, but that list had been changing a lot lately.

Sharpe left Emma and Aidan alone for a few minutes and returned with the news that Frost had hooked up the hayrack wagon for them and would be escorting them down to the bonfire.

"And we need an escort why?" she asked quietly, her cheeks flaming after she said the words.

"Ha!" Sharpe burst out. "Not the reason you're thinking. He's driving," Sharpe explained with a mischievous grin, "because there are too many family members to take in one trip. We're going along with Avery and Jake and their family because Jake wants to see the surprise."

"The surprise. The one you and Aidan were talking about?"

"Yep. The very one. It's right up Jake's alley and will give him a real hoot."

Emma had met Jake, and he'd seemed rather gregarious. She wondered what kind of surprise a grown man like Jake would enjoy.

She found out soon enough. They loaded

up into a wagon lined with hay bales, a shiny, regal-looking black horse ready to pull. Sharpe tucked himself in close to Emma and wrapped a wool blanket across their laps.

"To stay warm," he explained, but she didn't miss the look of interest at both of them that flashed from Avery's eyes.

Nothing to see here! It isn't like that, she wanted to say. There was nothing between her and Sharpe.

Except there was, no matter how hard she tried to deny it.

There *was* something between them, at least on her part.

Which was going to make leaving Whispering Pines all that much more difficult when the time came—and that time felt as if it was drawing nearer by the second.

"We're here at Aidan's special surprise," Sharpe suddenly announced. "Hop off, everyone."

Emma was amazed to discover they'd stopped in the middle of the road between the two pumpkin patches Sharpe had taken her to a couple of weeks ago by horse. Both of the patches were now sparse and appeared mostly trampled over.

Emma looked around, trying to discern why they were there. Whatever it was, Frost wasn't waiting for them to figure it out. He expertly turned the hayrack around and headed straight back for the barn without another word.

Aidan was so excited he was hopping from one leg to another, doing that dance of his. He grabbed her hand and practically dragged her to a tarp-covered...

Something.

"Go ahead, Aidan. Do the honors!" Sharpe encouraged.

With a whoop, Aidan untied the corners of the tarp and flipped it backward and off the large wooden object. It took Emma a few seconds to figure out what it was—a gigantic catapult. It looked like something out of medieval times.

"Aidan made this," Sharpe said, proudly slapping Aidan's back. "He had the idea for it, he drew up the plans for the wood and hardware, and he executed it all on his own. Hammer, saw, electric drill. You name it. He did it."

"I didn't even know you knew how to use a hammer," Emma said, gaping at the size of the catapult, which was a good three feet taller than she was.

"I took woodworking for one of my after-school classes," Aidan said. "I didn't like it very much, because we had to make stupid stuff like boxes and stools. We even had to make a pencil. How dumb is that? But making this was way cool, especially because I got to plan it out and draw it and everything."

"Never mind the woodworking," Jake said, admiring the catapult.

Aidan looked a little taken aback at Jake's quasi insult and Emma quickly stepped in, knowing Jake hadn't meant it the way it sounded.

"Jake's just kidding, aren't you, Jake?"

"Kidding? About what? You certainly showed off your woodworking skills right fine. But if this thing works like I think it's going to, we're talking about understanding some serious physics here, and that's really impressive for a boy your age."

"I have no doubt this thing is going to do exactly what it's supposed to do," Sharpe said, laying a hand on Aidan's shoulder and grinning down at him.

"Which is?" Emma asked the obvious

question, feeling as if everyone else here was in the know except her.

"Watch how it works!" Aidan exclaimed. He looked around on the ground for a moment before choosing the largest pumpkin he could find as Baloo barked at his heels. He carefully rolled the pumpkin into the leather sling, pulled back the lever until it clicked and then released it with a whoop of joy.

The pumpkin went soaring through the air, and Baloo chased it as if it were a gigantic tennis ball. He yipped and rolled out of the way just before the meteoric pumpkin plummeted back to earth with a splat, leaving seeds and guts everywhere. Somehow the dog managed not to get covered in goo, a feat Emma thought was equally amazing.

"Oh, yeah," Jake cheered. "That was awesome. Way to go, kid. Now it's my turn."

Aidan was grinning from ear to ear as he stepped aside to let Jake give it a go on his catapult machine.

"And what do you call this gizmo?" she asked her beaming brother, thinking it should be named after him. When scientists made up new medicines, they were always named after the scientist, right?

"It's a pumpkin launcher," Sharpe answered, sounding as if it should be obvious. "Remember how I told you all of my siblings have contributed in their own special way to Winslow's Woodlands? Well, thanks to Aidan, this is our special contribution. Next year we'll have it up and running so visitors can have a go at pumpkin launching."

"Since he was the one who had the idea and built the thing, I think you need to name it after Aidan," she suggested.

"Aidan's Aimer," Sharpe said. "What do you think of that, Aidan? Now every visitor who comes over here to sling a pumpkin will know you were the bright mind behind the catapult."

"With the goal being what?" she asked just as Jake's pumpkin came splatting ferociously to the ground, bouncing a few times before breaking into pieces. She could see what the catapult did. That was obvious. *Why* one would want to catapult a pumpkin was a whole other thing entirely.

"Yaassss!" Jake howled with delight and pumped his fist as the pumpkin spilled its guts.

"I should think that would be obvious,"

Sharpe said with a laugh. "Aidan created it to smash pumpkins."

"I see," Emma said, although she didn't. She really didn't. Smashing pumpkins was supposed to be a form of amusement?

She looked around her at all the happy smiles, little boys and grown men alike, and realized that out in the country, smashing pumpkins was a prime source of entertainment.

"Okay," she said, giving in with a giggle. "Let me grab a pumpkin so you can show me how to use this thing."

Sharpe was incredibly proud of Aidan for all the work he'd done. And although he could tell the pumpkin launcher had come as somewhat of a surprise to Emma, she'd been a good sport about it and had launched a few pumpkins of her own.

But now the sun was starting to set, and Frost was back with the hayrack, having already taken everyone else besides the few of them at the launcher to the site of the bonfire. Sharpe was really looking forward to this evening. He always enjoyed sharing bonfire evenings with his family, and tonight was extra special since Emma and Aidan were there with him.

With what he now knew about Emma and Aidan's background, it was important for him to share what it felt like to participate in a close family activity. He hoped they would leave Whispering Pines with permanent, heart-felt memories of their time here, even if the thought of them leaving squeezed at his heart.

By the time they arrived at the bonfire, someone had already lit the fire, and the flames were roaring two feet high in the pit, which was surrounded by large logs to sit on or lean against.

Emma breathed in audibly. "This is absolutely stunning," she murmured.

"I'm glad you think so," Sharpe responded, his chest warming at the expression on her face. "Have you ever had hot dogs cooked over an open flame?"

"Can't say that I have."

"You're in for a real treat," he assured her. "And s'mores?"

"Some more what? Hot dogs?"

He threw back his head and laughed. She was too cute for words, especially when her brow was knit with confusion.

Sharpe settled her not far from the roaring fire on a soft bed of pine needles with her back to a log and wrapped her in a green plaid woolen blanket, then called Aidan to his side. The boy bounded over with Baloo at his heel.

"Grab one of those branches that have the point carved on one end," he instructed Aidan. "See how they're green inside? Frost cut them from a spot nearby the creek bed. Because they're still fresh and green, they won't burn when we cook with them."

He showed Aidan how to thread a hot dog onto the stick and hold it over the open flame, enjoying the look of pure joy emanating from the boy's face as he cooked his own dinner. He'd come a long way from the kid who, when they'd first met, only wanted to keep his nose in his phone all the time and spent all his free time playing video games. Now he was enjoying everything the outdoors had to offer. He'd excelled at horsemanship with Diamond, and his pumpkin launcher was brilliant.

Sharpe hoped he wasn't doing Emma a disservice by mentoring Aidan in all ways mountain and farm living. That wasn't his intention, by any means. But he wanted to show

Aidan some happiness while he was here in Whispering Pines, and he'd really bonded with the young man—probably more so than he should have. Even so, Aidan had learned skills he'd be able to take with him throughout the rest of his life, even in the city.

Without even being told, Aidan found himself a place by the fire, Baloo tucked up right beside him as he ate. Sharpe noticed Gramps and Emma's nan sitting on a nearby log, sharing a blanket around their shoulders and quietly talking. The way they gazed at each other with pure appreciation made Sharpe swallow hard and look away, feeling as if he was interrupting something special between the two elderly people.

"You want me to prepare your hot dog for you?" Sharpe asked Emma, ready to perform his gentlemanly duty, which he imagined would feel to Emma similar to threading a worm on a hook.

"Absolutely not," she exclaimed. "This will be my one and only opportunity to cook a hot dog over an open fire. I'm in it for the *whole* experience."

He raised his eyebrows and nodded. "I'm impressed."

"I may look like a city girl on the outside, but I imagine I can cook a hot dog over an open flame at least as well as you can."

"Oh, we're *so* on." He grabbed a stick of his own and jammed a hot dog onto the pointed end. He was going to show her how a cowboy cooked a dog.

Unfortunately for him, he was all too aware of Emma by his side—her smile, her laughter and the light floral scent that was uniquely hers that teased his senses. His mind wandered as he watched her expertly cook her hot dog.

"Um… Sharpe?" Emma's amused voice penetrated through his mental haze.

He looked up and locked eyes with her. She was definitely entertained by something.

She pointed at the end of his stick. "Your hot dog is burning."

"Augh!" He pulled the now-charbroiled hot dog away from the fire and blew on it to extinguish the flame. He'd been distracted admiring Emma and had managed to put the end of his stick directly in the middle of the fire, and now his hot dog was black and inedible. He groaned and pushed it off his stick with the toe of his boot, kicking it into the fire.

Emma, on the other hand, was placing her

perfectly cooked hot dog in a bun on a nearby plate and adding ketchup and mustard.

"I win," she jested, grinning widely. "Here. Allow me." She expertly threaded a second hot dog onto her stick and cooked it to perfection before placing it in the bun on his plate.

"Not a word," he warned her with a mock scowl as he added a big dollop of spicy mustard across the top of the hot dog.

"I wouldn't think of it," she answered. "I wasn't about to point out that perfection comes easy to me."

"Not fair. I was distracted."

She raised a dark auburn eyebrow over a twinkling eye. "Were you, now?"

"I'd call for a rematch, but Frost is tuning up his guitar."

"I didn't realize music was part of the bonfire," she said.

"Of course. Anywhere Frost goes, music follows. Besides, no bonfire is complete without camp songs. Stick around and you may even see more surprising things. I promise you won't be bored."

"I've already been surprised a hundred times today. And now you're saying there's more?"

"Oh, yes," he assured her. "There's more. Much more."

And then he took a bite of his hot dog, which he had to admit, if only to himself, had been perfectly cooked over the open fire. It was delicious, much better than any he'd ever cooked.

Because Emma had cooked it, and the more time he spent with her, the more amazed he was by this woman who could stand up for herself and yet be sweet and tender all at the same time.

How could he not admire her?

Chapter Seven

Emma was enjoying every single second of the bonfire, from the hayrack ride that had brought them there to the pleasant way Sharpe and his brother and sisters and their families interacted with each other. There was no shortage of smiles and laughter, giggling from the small children and Baloo's happy barking as he played around with Aidan in the background, out of the way of the fire.

When Frost first pulled out his guitar, he quietly strummed acoustic tunes in the background, perfect for sharing a meal. But it wasn't long before he changed things around and started playing and singing a familiar tune about the Colorado Rocky Mountains, and the Winslows quickly picked it up and sang along. Emma vaguely remembered the song, as it was a classic country song that almost everyone knew, but she didn't immediately join in with the singing. Rather, she just listened, starting with Frost's amazing tenor, and then the sisters and their husbands adding harmony. Finally, Sharpe came in with his warm, rich baritone that felt as if it almost completed the chords.

She didn't know why, but Emma wouldn't have guessed Sharpe to be a singer. Yet she really enjoyed listening to his voice in song. Emma had never heard anything like what the Winslows were creating. It was as if they'd all been born to harmonize together. Frost moved from country to a well-known hymn without missing a beat, and the Winslows followed him with equal ease.

Sharpe reached out and took her hand, threading their fingers as he squeezed it lightly. He caught her gaze in the firelight and silently urged her to add her voice. Even Aidan was singing, which surprised Emma, because she hadn't known he could sing, either, much less where he would have learned "Amazing Grace." She highly doubted her parents had ever taken him to church or even dropped him off at the local Sunday school.

She made a mental note to ask him later where he'd learned the hymn. In the meantime, she softly and a little bit nervously added her own voice to the mix. She didn't really know where she fitted in, so she simply sang the melody.

She was surprised at how easy it was to feel as if she were truly a part of this family, as if she belonged here with them.

If only that were true.

They sang a few more songs, then Frost took a quick break so they could all make their s'mores. Emma hadn't known what she'd been missing. Who would ever have guessed that roasting a marshmallow and smushing it between graham crackers with a square of chocolate could taste this good? It was truly an evening she would never forget, for it wasn't likely she would ever again have the opportunity to roast a marshmallow over an open fire.

She couldn't seem to hold on to her flailing emotions. It felt as if she was on a roller coaster, flying high one moment and plunging down the next when she remembered she'd soon be leaving.

As soon as she'd finished her s'more and

cleaned off her sticky fingers, she reached for Sharpe's hand, needing to feel his presence close to her. She would enjoy tonight, she decided, and face tomorrow when it came.

When Frost again picked up his guitar, Jake started in clapping, stomping and chanting. "Sharpe, Sharpe, Sharpe, Sharpe, Sharpe." Within moments, everyone around the fire was likewise asking for Sharpe to do—

What?

Emma turned curiously toward Sharpe. He winked and stood, making a big deal out of stretching as if in preparation for a run.

"Hey, Aidan, can I borrow Baloo for a moment?" he asked.

At the sound of his name, the dog barked in response and ran to Sharpe's side, clearly ready to participate in whatever Sharpe had in mind.

As Frost expertly fingered the guitar strings to produce a country classic, Sharpe crouched with one knee to the earth and tipped his cowboy hat low with his fingers, staring at the ground. To Emma's surprise, Baloo seemed to know exactly what he was expected to do and put his front paws on Sharpe's back.

As the music intensified, Sharpe stood and

bowed toward Baloo, who play bowed back at him. Emma was completely enthralled as Sharpe hooked his thumbs through his belt loops and started dancing, boot-scooting his way around the outside of the bonfire with Baloo weaving his way in and out of Sharpe's ankles. Sharpe made a hoop with his arms, and Baloo jumped through without missing a beat.

Sharpe picked his hat off his head and rolled onto his back in the dirt, his boots in the air, flattened so Baloo could balance on them and carefully turn in a circle before bounding back to the ground. Sharpe jumped back on his feet in one quick movement like the athlete he was and continued the dance, using his arms and legs to interact with Baloo. The excited border collie barked in delight as the two of them made figure eights and Baloo once again jumped through Sharpe's hooped arms. As the music came to a close, Sharpe swept off his hat and bowed first to Baloo, who returned his action with another play bow, and then to his captive audience, who clapped and hooted their enthusiasm.

"Come on up, Aidan, and see what you can do with Baloo," Sharpe suggested, gesturing toward the border collie.

Aidan laughed and jumped to his feet, dashing toward Baloo. When he reached the dog, he took his front paws in his hands and danced side to side in time with the upbeat song Frost was now playing.

"It's about time the rest of us get to join in," Gramps complained, standing and pulling Nan up with him. He might be eighty, but as far as Emma was concerned, he had some serious game, and it wasn't long before he had Nan's waist wrapped securely in his free arm, balancing with his cane in the other. Considering Nan also had a cane, they barely moved as they rocked back and forth together, but Emma supposed that wasn't the point when it came to this adorable pair. Anyone with eyes could see how hard they were crushing on each other.

"You have the right idea, Gramps," Jake said with a whoop. "Come on, girlie. Dance with your daddy." He picked up his daughter and swung her around until she was giggling with delight. Their toddler son was sound asleep in Avery's lap, but she was quietly laughing at her husband's antics.

A man like Jake would drive Emma crazy, but he was just right for Avery, and it warmed

Emma's heart to see. Truly, all of the Winslow sisters had God-given marriages, something Emma hadn't given much thought to until lately but which suddenly was on her mind. Emma could see how well everyone all got along, both as couples and together as one large extended family. She'd never experienced anything like it before and knew she probably wouldn't experience it again in the future.

The Winslows were a unique family, loving and—

"Are you going to make me stand here all night?" Sharpe demanded.

She'd been so lost in her thoughts she hadn't realized Sharpe was standing right in front of her, his arm extended to her.

"Oh, no." Heat rose to her face. "I'm not a dancer. I trip over my own two feet."

"Now, I know that's not true. I've seen you in high heels. But even if it were, that's okay. I'll lead."

"Dancing and wearing heels is not the same thing. Don't say I didn't warn you."

She stood, feeling awkward as he led her to an empty spot around the bonfire. At least everyone else appeared not to be paying them all that much attention. He took her hands and placed them on his broad shoulders, then gently put his hands around her waist.

"That's all there is to it," he whispered as he smiled down at her and rocked from side to side.

At first, she couldn't even breathe from his nearness, and then when she did, she felt dizzy from the scent of him—earth and evergreen and leather. It was intoxicating in a way she'd never before experienced.

And he was right. It wasn't difficult to dance with him. His strong arms were tender, and he swayed exactly on the beat of the music, making it easy for her to follow.

After a few minutes, he pulled her closer, tucking her head against his chest. She listened to the beat of his heart, which was thrumming in time to her own.

For the second time this evening, she wished she could bottle the moment and keep it forever. Nearly everyone was up dancing now, from small children to Gramps and Nan and even Aidan and the dog. The feeling of belonging, of being truly embraced by this lovely family, was almost more than Emma could bear.

And that was nothing compared to the feelings growing in her heart for Sharpe. Who would have guessed the sullen, intimidating cowboy she'd first met a few weeks ago would turn out to have a heart of gold? And, for no good reason except that he was an empathetic individual who really cared, that he would take it upon himself to become Aidan's mentor? That he would welcome her to a family event, no doubt understanding how much it meant to her to see how a real family interacted.

Or did he?

She leaned back and locked her gaze with his. His eyes were midnight blue in the flickering firelight, and her breath caught in her throat. She wasn't sure she could speak. But she somehow forced air through her lungs.

"Thank you." Her voice broke under the strain of her dry throat.

He cracked a gentle half smile as his eyebrows rose underneath his hat. "For what, darlin'?"

"For sharing your world with me and Aidan. You'll never know how much it means to us to have this time with you."

She glanced over at Aidan, who'd returned

to his seat, Baloo curled up next to him with his head on the boy's lap. Sharpe followed her gaze.

Without warning, he held his arm out and twirled her underneath it, pulling her back into his embrace before he spoke.

"Whatever you think I've done for you, just know that you and Aidan have done twice as much for me. God blessed me the day you two walked into my life."

"I wish…" Emma started, then abruptly came to a stop.

She wished the night would never end.

She wished she could stay in Whispering Pines longer.

She wished her life were different, so she could make her own choices.

She wished she could follow her dream of owning her own business and not have to keep working at a job she didn't love.

She wished she could pursue a serious relationship with the best man she'd ever had the pleasure of knowing.

But what good is wishing?

The reality was, she was Aidan's guardian, and she had to do what was best for him. That meant going back to her job in LA, where she had a decent salary and great benefits, where she'd be able to find a good place for Aidan to attend school.

She sighed, understanding the unfortunate truth even if she wished it weren't so.

Reality trumped wishes every time.

Sharpe had been anticipating this day ever since they'd visited Mongoose's homeless shelter and he'd told Emma about his friend David. Today, he was taking Emma and Aidan to visit David on his sheep farm, to show Aidan yet another interesting part of country life and Emma what could happen when a homeless veteran found a new meaning for his life.

Because it was early November in Colorado, there was snow on the ground, where it would stay until spring. Though she was still a woman any man would look at twice, Emma had finally given up her high fashion for clothes that were more suitable for the Colorado mountains in winter—a white puffer jacket over a light green sweater, jeans and white snow boots, white knit gloves, and the cutest light green beanie hat with a little poof ball on top that bobbed every time she turned her head.

Aidan was in the back seat of the truck with Baloo tucked up next to him. As usual, the boy appeared distant as he listened to his music with his earbuds. Sharpe was finally starting to get used to having to gain the boy's attention with a wave or a gesture before speaking.

The thought made him chuckle. He was really starting to care for the boy, probably much more than he should.

As he pulled up the long driveway to David's farm, he saw his friend waving from the porch with his left arm. Sharpe knew when they got closer, Emma and Aidan would be able to see the wounds of war. David wore a prosthetic right arm. It didn't stop him from living his best life, but it had taken David a long and painful period of time to find that life.

After parking in front of the house, Sharpe walked around the front of his truck and opened the doors for Emma and Aidan, who bounded out with the dog. As soon as he was out of the truck, Baloo ran directly to the similar-looking border collie standing guard next to David's leg, and the two dogs immediately started barking at each other and playing together, rolling about in the snow. Aidan laughed and ran to follow them.

"How are you doing, my friend?" he asked, clasping David's left hand and bumping shoulders with him.

"Looks like Blue is doing well," David said as Sharpe embraced him into a full hug.

Sharpe nodded. "It's Baloo now. He's become Aidan's sidekick, and Aidan has learned a lot about the use of therapy dogs through him. I thought he'd enjoy meeting Baloo's brother and seeing yet another way border collies can work."

"You said they're brothers?" Emma asked.

"They are," David affirmed. "Blue— *Baloo*—and Axel were in the same litter. Axel was the runt. I couldn't resist. Sharpe and his sisters taught him to be my service dog, which I'm grateful for. He helps me with my PTSD and makes doing some things with my arm easier, like turning lights on and off and opening and closing doors for me."

"It sounds as if it didn't hurt Axel to be the runt of the litter," Emma said.

"No, not at all. Of course, Sharpe picked the best and brightest to begin with, as I can see he is still in the habit of doing—even with the ladies." He laughed jovially and nodded toward Emma.

"I'm sorry, David," Sharpe immediately apologized. "I should have introduced you right away. This is my friend Emma."

He didn't know why he'd said that Emma was his *friend* and immediately wanted to take the words back. He didn't want David to think Emma was fair game in the dating department. He and his friend had always been competitive that way.

Then again, it wasn't as if he had any claim to her. Besides, she was leaving soon.

Even so, his feelings were getting more mixed up with every day that passed. He knew they were growing stronger despite his best efforts to put them aside.

"I'm happy to meet you, David. My brother and I are super excited to see your sheep farm," Emma said enthusiastically. She held out her right hand to shake his, and to Sharpe's astonishment, she didn't flinch or even blink when she shook David's prosthetic hand, as many people would have.

But then again, that was his Emma.

Well, not *his* Emma.

"I'd be happy to show you around. I own

about two hundred and fifty acres here. It's taken me a few years to build up my herd to be profitable. But I don't require much. God's been good to me and has given me everything I need to survive and enjoy life. I get to ride my horse and my ATV and appreciate the Colorado land and weather."

"Colorado has been a wonderful experience for me," Emma said. "I was born and raised in a suburb of Chicago, and we got lots of snow there. But for the past eleven years, I've lived in Southern California, so experiencing snow again is a real treat for me."

"California, huh? What brings you up to Whispering Pines, then?"

"Long story," Sharpe interrupted, giving her an out if she wanted one. She caught his eye and wordlessly thanked him for stepping in.

"Just family matters," Emma answered vaguely. "My grandmother lives in town. Sharpe said you two were best friends in high school?"

It was clearly an attempt at a change of subject, and Emma looked tense until David answered.

"Yes, we played football together."

Emma looked relieved that David followed

her train of thought, but if David noticed, he didn't let on.

"Did he tell you I tried to get him to enlist in the army with me?" David continued.

"You know I couldn't," Sharpe said, feeling that oh-so-familiar stab of guilt whenever the subject was brought up. What would have happened if he'd chosen to abandon his responsibilities and entered the military with David instead? Could he maybe have saved him from losing his arm? Or from ending up on the streets on drugs?

He knew those kinds of thoughts didn't do anyone any good. The past was the past and couldn't be changed even if he wanted to. He'd made the best decision he could at the time. There was no sense rehashing it, so he purposefully pushed those thoughts away.

"That's my friend," David said, patting Sharpe's shoulder affectionately. "Always taking care of everyone. He may have wanted to enlist with me, but he had to stay behind to take care of his family. They needed him. And he did a good job at that, didn't he? The Winslow family has thrived, and Winslow's Woodlands is a total success by every measure."

"It certainly is. He's made a real difference out there," Emma agreed.

"I also took Emma and Aidan out to meet Mongoose and volunteer at the shelter," Sharpe said.

Emma's gaze widened in surprise. Perhaps she thought he wouldn't bring up such a touchy subject with David, given what she knew of his friend's past, but Sharpe thought David would want to know.

"Is that a fact?" David replied, turning his attention to Emma. "What did you think of the old coot?"

"If you're referring to Mongoose, I liked him very much," Emma replied with a smile. "And there's nothing old about him. He's in perfect shape, and I wouldn't want to meet him in a dark alley."

"I'll say," David agreed. "Did they tell you how he got his name?"

"Sharpe told me," Emma said. "And I believe him."

"You and me both," David said. "I feel sorry for any snake that gets in his way."

"Mongoose isn't the only one with a nickname at the shelter," Sharpe said proudly.

"Emma managed to pick one up after just one day."

"Really? I'm intrigued." David crossed his good arm over his chest.

"It's not that big of a deal," Emma said, gesturing with her hand. "Honestly."

"It's a big deal to the men who were there that day. They christened her the Coffee Lady. She took it upon herself to make sure everyone had a hot mug of coffee, and she even filled their thermoses for them."

"The next time she goes back, you ought to get her a T-shirt that says Coffee Lady."

Emma's face instantly fell, and her look pierced right into Sharpe's heart.

"I'm afraid that as much as I want to, I won't be going back to visit. I really loved helping out at the shelter, but unfortunately, I have to return to California in two weeks to go back to work."

"After Thanksgiving, though, right?" Sharpe asked, holding his breath for the answer. They hadn't yet talked specifics.

"Yes. The Saturday after Thanksgiving."

"Then you'll be sharing Thanksgiving dinner with the Winslows," David said, more of a statement than a question.

"Oh, no, I—" she started, but Sharpe jumped in before she could finish.

"Of course she is. My gramps has already invited the whole Fitzpatrick family. He's crushing on Emma's nan, which is hilarious. And, David, you know you're always welcome at our table."

"You know how much I enjoy spending time with you guys, but Mom has invited me down to Oklahoma for dinner this year."

"Nice."

"Yeah. My brother and his wife and their two little ones are going to be there, as well. I don't get to see my nephews as often as I'd like, so I'm really looking forward to it."

Sharpe knew how much David wanted a family of his own and said a quick prayer that David's Thanksgiving with his extended family would go well. It was tough to see your siblings married and settled down when you weren't, which wasn't something Sharpe had given much thought to until recently. For most of his life it hadn't bothered him at all, but lately, thoughts of a wife and kids had crept into his mind, surprising him with their intensity.

Thanksgiving Day, though, was going to be

great for Emma, especially since she wanted
to go back to the shelter one more time. She
didn't yet know she'd actually have the opportunity to visit, as the Winslows made a
practice of serving a Thanksgiving meal for
the veterans before returning home for turkey with all the fixings.

"Do you want to go see the sheep?" David
asked Emma, and she nodded enthusiastically. David whistled, and Axel immediately
returned to his side at a run, quickly followed
by Baloo and then Aidan. Sharpe got a kick
out of that.

Chapter Eight

❧

They walked over to the nearest field behind David's farmhouse, where a small herd of sheep loitered against the far fence, each one of them dotted with a spot of blue or green paint. Emma wondered if they were going to have to walk all the way up the hill to the far side of the fence in order to better see the sheep. As it was now, they'd need binoculars to get a close look.

"You paint your sheep?" she asked, amused. "White isn't your color?" How, she wondered, did he choose which ones he wanted to paint green and which to paint blue?

"Well, technically I only dab paint on the rams' bellies. I've got two rams, so that's why there's green and blue. That way I know which ewes are going to be mamas soon, so

I can herd them into the nearest pasture for birthing. I like to keep a close eye on the expecting ewes. It's something I learned on a trip to Ireland, and I decided to follow their practice here, since I have a small acreage and flock. It's not the most common way to follow pregnant ewes, but it works perfectly for me."

"That's fascinating," Emma said, but then she glanced down at her feet. "I think perhaps I've worn the wrong boots, though, which seems to be a bad habit of mine. These are my snow boots, but it looks as if we're going to be doing quite a bit of hiking to get up close to the sheep."

Sharpe chuckled. "Now, this is why I really brought you to check out David's sheep farm today. David is about to astound you. And it won't matter at all what kind of footwear you've got on for a change."

"Well," said David. "I'm not really the one who is going to amaze you. It's the dogs who do all of the hard work. But it's still quite something to see if you're not familiar with the process."

"Aidan?" Sharpe called to the boy, who was still lingering back with the dogs. "Come watch and see what David can do with Axel and Baloo."

Aidan came to stand near Sharpe, and he put an affectionate hand on the boy's shoulder.

Emma was intrigued. Though she knew little about dog breeds, she knew enough to know border collies were herding animals. But how that would play out, she hadn't a clue.

David put his thumb and forefinger of his left hand to his lips and whistled three short bursts.

Whee, whee, wheet.

Both dogs immediately rushed to spots directly in front of him and sat, their eyes upon David as if expecting their next command. He had their full attention, their gazes on his face.

Next, he blew two short, even whistles.

"That sound tells the dogs to walk up, meaning to approach the flock of sheep," David explained as the dogs turned and bolted toward the flock. David then made one long, low whistle, and both dogs dropped to a lie-down position, their eyes following the sheep but not making a move until David told them to do so.

Emma was completely enthralled by David's presentation and how well the dogs were responding to the whistled commands.

"That'll do," David told the border collies when they'd herded the whole flock of sheep to the front fence. "Y'all are good boys." He scrubbed behind each of the dogs' ears and turned to see how Emma and Aidan had enjoyed the production.

"That was ah-mazing! Baloo rocks!" Aidan exclaimed, jumping up and down and doing his unique wiggling dance, his arms and legs going every which way.

"Baloo is quite an amazing dog," Sharpe agreed. "Axel, too. We have two rocking dogs."

"And David rocks most of all," Emma said, beaming at Sharpe's friend. "The dogs wouldn't have known what to do without him there to tell them when to move and when to stop, never mind which direction to turn the flock. I've never seen anything like it."

David's face turned cherry red under his blond beard. "The dogs know what they're doing all on their own," he said, scrubbing a nervous hand down his face. "They could do it without me. I think they just allow me to take part so I feel better about myself."

Sharpe snorted. "Is it working?"

"Sharpe!" Emma exclaimed.

"He's only jealous because he can't whistle himself," David said with a laugh. He turned to Sharpe and grinned. "Do you remember trying to learn how to whistle at the girls when we were in junior high? I picked it up right away, but you never did."

Now Sharpe's face was as heated as David's. For some reason, it reminded Emma of all those nature documentaries she'd seen where two males of a species would face off against each other to impress a nearby female. It amused her—and surprised her—that *she* was the nearby female. Yet it was clear they were vying for her attention.

"Let's hear it," Emma insisted. She probably shouldn't be egging them on, but she couldn't seem to help herself.

"Hear what?" Sharpe asked, tipping up his chin.

"Your whistle, of course. Can you send Baloo running across the field after the sheep?"

He stared at her a moment, his lips pressed together. It was only when the stare turned into a glare that Emma wondered if she'd gone too far.

"I can't do it," he finally admitted. "David

is right. I've never gotten the hang of whistling, not in all these years. But whistling at women is demeaning, anyway, don't you think? So what's the point of learning?"

"Depends on who's doing the whistling," Emma said with a laugh. "While I don't want to be whistled at by a complete stranger, I'm not entirely opposed to a good-looking guy I already know expressing his appreciation with a whistle."

Sharpe's still-pressed lips curled downward into a deep frown, and his eyebrows furrowed.

"I'm just kidding," she said, trying to backtrack. It seemed to her as if Sharpe's feelings—or at least his ego—were really hurt over this simple thing, and she hadn't meant for that to happen. "In the scheme of things, whistling doesn't seem to be the most important skill a man needs to have—unless he's a sheep farmer like David. And you could use a plastic whistle if it came to that, couldn't you? You do plenty of things well, Sharpe—like mentoring my brother, for example. I don't think there's a better, stronger man alive to have taken Aidan under his wing."

That seemed to do the trick. Sharpe's posture relaxed and his smile returned.

David affectionately slapped Sharpe's shoulder. "That's amazing, buddy. Really. I can see how much the kid admires you."

"He likes Sharpe a lot more than he likes me, I'm afraid, and I'm both his sister and his guardian," Emma said with a laugh.

It was meant to be a joke.

And yet…

Aidan had really bonded with Sharpe. Which gave Emma legitimate concerns about what would happen when they moved away from Whispering Pines. She suspected Aidan wasn't going to like California nearly as much as Colorado. Yet the same barriers existed that had been there since the first day she'd entered town. No matter how she personally felt about it, her job in LA could support them better than anything she could get in a small mountain town, she was sure.

If only there was another option, one that would make everyone happy.

One where she could see what might happen between her and Sharpe. As it was, she had to keep those walls around her heart firmly guarded. And that was getting harder and harder with every day that passed.

Sharpe was proud of David for all the progress he'd made, fighting his way out of despair, but he couldn't help but want Emma's pretty smile aimed at him. This had been David's moment to shine, and he wouldn't get in the way of that, despite the way his ego was hollering in the background to keep Emma's attention firmly planted on him. After all, they were here so Emma could meet David and hear his story from his own lips.

"Anyone want a cup of coffee?" David offered.

"Aidan, keep an eye on the dogs for us, will you?" Sharpe called to the boy as the adults went inside and settled at the kitchen table. Sharpe took the seat next to Emma, casually draping his arm over the back of her chair. If David noticed, so be it.

And if Emma noticed? Well…

"I imagine Sharpe has told you my story," David said as he poured the three of them steaming mugs of coffee. "Sugar or cream, Emma?"

"Sharpe's told me some things," Emma said. "Sugar, please."

David poured Sharpe's coffee without asking, already knowing he took his Colorado dark roast black. Nothing sweet needed to be added to make it the way he liked it.

David slipped into the seat opposite Sharpe and Emma and took a tentative sip of his brew, then grinned across at Emma.

"What else would you like to know?"

"I'm not here to interrogate you," Emma protested, pressing a hand to her throat. "Honestly, we came to meet you and see the sheep, not dig into your personal business."

"But Sharpe has told you my story. Or part of it, at least?"

"Yes," Sharpe intervened bluntly. "I told you we've visited Mongoose. Emma saw how the homeless veterans were living. I thought it would be good for her to hear a personal story, and yours has a more positive outcome than many. So I thought it would be good for her to hear your story straight from you. You tell it better than I do."

Which was true. David was much more outgoing than Sharpe and had a gift for storytelling.

"Okay, then. Where to begin?" He paused and smiled. "I enlisted in the army even before I finished high school. As I'm sure Sharpe told you, I tried to get him to sign up with me, but he didn't. Said he couldn't. Some best friend he is, huh?"

Sharpe saw the dismay cross Emma's features, and guilt once again stabbed at him.

"Thank you for your service," Emma said, straight to the point, her gaze meeting David's. "We need people like you defending our country, and I appreciate everything you've sacrificed."

David cracked a half smile. "I did what I could."

"It seems to me you did more than that," Emma said. "Don't downplay what you've done."

"If you're referring to my arm—I knew what I was getting into when I signed my name on my enlistment papers. I didn't go in blind. And I certainly knew what to expect after I'd gone through basic training and was deployed for duty. It was my job, and I was happy to do it."

"But you lost your arm, and much more

than that for a while. You ended up on the streets."

"That's true. But it wasn't my arm that pushed me into taking illegal drugs. I felt I'd lost my reason for existing when I could no longer be deployed. I'd defined myself as a soldier all my adult life, and suddenly that was taken away from me, and I didn't know what to do. I self-medicated so I didn't have to feel anything. When I had to choose between paying rent and getting high, I started living on the streets. At first, it seemed like a reasonable answer—at least, until winter came."

"And then you met Mongoose?"

"I remember the night it happened, even though I was high on drugs at the time. It was an especially cold night, and I wasn't sure where I was going to sleep where I wouldn't quite literally freeze to death. I was walking around the streets downtown, praying God would somehow save me from myself. Suddenly, Mongoose was right there in front of me, wrapping me in a warm coat and leading me back to his shelter. I immediately recognized a fellow soldier in Mongoose, even before he told me he was Delta Force. I'm not sure I would have allowed him to lead me back to his shelter if it weren't for that."

David sighed and tapped his prosthetic hand against the table. Sharpe glanced at Emma, who was looking at David's hand with curiosity, but not in a way that would make him feel uneasy.

"Mongoose allowed me to stay until the snowstorm passed and then helped me get into rehab. I was ready to get off the streets by then. He asked me if I had anyone I wanted to contact. I was too ashamed to reach out to my family, so I gave him Sharpe's number."

To Sharpe's surprise, Emma reached out her hand and placed it over Sharpe's, giving it a light squeeze.

"Sharpe started volunteering at Mongoose's shelter regularly when I was in rehab. By the time I got out, I was prepared to find a job and a place to live. Sharpe knew me better than anyone, and when he heard about this little place being for sale, he suggested I try sheep farming. He knew I needed somewhere I could find peace and quiet after all I'd been through, someplace I could get back in touch with God. This place has been perfect for me."

"I can tell," Emma murmured with a kind smile. "You definitely seem at peace here. And I know what you mean about Sharpe. You couldn't ask for a better friend. He's helped Aidan and me in so many ways since we've come to town."

"Really?" David threw back his head and laughed. "I wonder how you managed that?" he asked, verbally poking at his friend. "No—I take that back. I think I can figure it out."

David's green eyes were gleaming with mischief.

Don't you even, Sharpe thought, though he didn't speak what he was thinking. If David started teasing him, Sharpe was afraid he was going to be slinking out of the kitchen in thorough mortification.

Thankfully, David didn't follow through with the thoughts clearly going through his head, although he did continue to look between Sharpe and Emma with a knowing smile on his face.

"Did Sharpe tell you about the pumpkin catapult he and Aidan made? He said he's been looking for the perfect way to add his own special touch to Winslow's Woodlands, and that was it. I'm sure you'd probably love hurling and smashing pumpkins as much as the rest of the male population around here seems to. You should come over sometime and try it."

"His special touch, huh?" David said, raising a blond eyebrow. "I thought that was only supposed to happen once a Winslow tied the knot. Is there something you two aren't telling me?" He grinned and looked directly at Emma's left hand.

Emma's gaze widened, and Sharpe swallowed hard around the lump in his throat. "It was all Aidan," Sharpe protested when he could finally form words. "He came up with the idea, planned it out on paper and built it all himself."

"And somehow that's supposed to convince me there's nothing special going on here?" David said with a laugh.

Emma was now gaping, not at David, but at Sharpe, her expression clearly expecting him to somehow talk his way out of this mess.

"Emma and Aidan are returning to LA just after Thanksgiving."

"Yes," Emma said, looking relieved. "I have to get back to work at the marketing agency," Emma continued. "I've used up all my paid time off and family leave just to take care of things here."

"I see. Well, that's good, I guess," David said, although he sounded questionable about the subject.

Sharpe was feeling the same way. He wasn't relieved that Emma was going. Quite the opposite. But he had no idea how to convince her she had any reason to stay.

Chapter Nine

Seeing David at his sheep farm had been another eye-opening experience for Emma, not only because the way he'd worked his sheep with the border collies had been nothing short of amazing, but because she'd gotten to see the special relationship between Sharpe and his best friend. She was so grateful God had rescued David from his time on the streets. How awful that must have been for him.

More than that, though, was the feeling she'd had during the time she and Sharpe had visited David that there was more to her relationship with him than mere friendship. She'd been physically attracted to Sharpe since the moment she'd met him, even when she'd only seen him as a surly, intimidating cowboy, but now that she knew what he was really like, that heart of gold he tried so hard to hide, she cared for him even more.

She had no idea if he felt the same way toward her, but what difference did it make when she was leaving in two weeks?

Her heart plummeted.

Was it awful that she was grieving more over having to leave Whispering Pines, the Winslow family and most especially Sharpe than she had over the deaths of her parents?

Did that make her a bad person—that she enjoyed living with and caring for her nan, who would never admit she needed any help?

And what about Aidan? He loved it here. He'd gone from a sullen city boy to a care-free country kid in just a matter of weeks. How would he react to living again in a small, claustrophobic city apartment where they couldn't have a yard, much less a dog? She had the feeling he was going to hate his new life almost as much as she disliked thinking about what her future was going to look like.

But what if it could be different? Was there any way she could change their future?

It gave her pause to think and pray.

This evening she was casually dressed in jeans and a white knit Aran sweater. Her calf-high boots had heels, but only an inch high, and they were block heels, so it was easy for her to walk in the couple of inches of fresh snow that covered the ground. For some reason known only to Nan, she had insisted they walk the short distance down the main street to get to Sally's Pizza, even though she had to use a walker to do so.

"The weather is perfect for walking tonight," she'd said.

Emma knew never to argue with Nan when she had her mind set on something.

It probably had something to do with Gramps, but she wasn't going to push the subject and spoil Nan's fun. She'd really come alive lately, and Emma was thrilled for her.

All the Winslows were meeting at Sally's Pizza for open mic night, where Frost would be performing, and they'd invited Nan, Aidan and Emma to hear him play. The Winslow clan took up most of the restaurant just between all the siblings and their families.

As soon as she entered with Nan, Sharpe's gramps appeared to whisk her away into a far corner, where he'd reserved a table so they'd have some privacy. Those two lovebirds put everyone else to shame, and there was no shortage of teasing from the bantering Winslow family.

Moments later, she saw Sharpe waving her over to a table close to the platform where Frost would be performing.

"Can I go play in the arcade?" Aidan asked, pulling on the fabric of Emma's sleeve. He was referring to the old-fashioned game room on the opposite side of Sally's Pizza.

"Sure. Come back when you get hungry, okay? Pepperoni, right?"

"Yep. And extra cheese," he exclaimed, then headed back toward the arcade with money he'd earned himself working for Sharpe.

"Wow. It's already noisy in here," she said, sliding into the booth opposite Sharpe. "We're right next to the platform, and it's still going to be hard to hear Frost play."

"They've got a good speaker system," he assured her. "It's always noisy when my family is around. It doesn't matter where we are—we'll increase the volume tenfold. And it's not even the kids making all the racket." He gestured toward Jake, who was howling with laughter over something Avery had said.

"What do you and Aidan want to eat?" Sharpe asked. "I'm buying."

"You don't have to do that," she said, her face heating.

His smile made his eyes gleam in the low lighting. "I know I don't have to. I want to. Now, what's your and Aidan's favorite kind of pizza?"

"Aidan likes pepperoni with extra cheese. I'll have a go at the salad bar."

"We're at a pizza joint and you're eating salad? Don't even tell me you're on a diet, because you definitely don't need to be." He smiled at her.

"No, no diet," she assured him. "And I absolutely like pizza. I'm just feeling like a salad tonight, and that salad bar looks fresh and full of goodies."

"It is. Sally stocks it with the best."

"Great, then. I'm sold. What are you getting?"

"Everything and the Kitchen Sink, minus anchovies," he answered.

She laughed.

"No, really. That's what the pizza is called. Everything and the Kitchen Sink."

"That's clever."

"That's Sally."

Speaking of Sally, she appeared just then at

their table, taking their food and drink orders. "I saw Nan and Gramps over there," she said with a hoot of laughter. "Looks to me like they're giving you two a run for your money."

"I'm sorry—what?" asked Emma, confused.

Sharpe groaned and hid his face in his hand. "Don't ask."

"Don't bother denying it, Sharpe Michael Winslow." Sally wagged a finger at him. "I've known you since you were knee-high to a grasshopper, and I've never seen a smile like the one that plastered all over your face the moment Emma walked in the door."

Emma felt embarrassed to be caught out this way, but she had to laugh at how Sharpe looked as if he wanted to hide under the table.

"Maybe if you say it a little louder, everyone in the whole restaurant will hear," Sharpe complained. Emma noticed he didn't try to deny his feelings, only throw Sally's words back at her.

"Honey, everyone here already knows. Your secret is out. The only ones who are pulling the wool over your eyes are the two of you."

She playfully swatted him on the head with

her order pad, then made her way back to the kitchen, where her husband did the cooking.

Emma practically gawked after her.

Sharpe laid his palms flat on the table and stared down at them. His face was flaming a bright red. "Well," he said, and then took a breath. "That just happened."

"It bothers you that much to be seen with me?" she teased.

"Yes… No! I was afraid she was embarrassing you when she implied that we were a couple."

"It doesn't bother me," she admitted in such a low voice she wasn't sure if he'd hear her or not. And she wasn't about to repeat herself. It had taken all her gumption to say the words once.

"Really?" He looked up and caught her gaze, his own glinting in the low overhead lighting. "You don't care if…" He swallowed so hard his Adam's apple bobbed. "…if everyone thinks we're together?"

"As long as it doesn't bother you, I don't see where the state of our relationship is anyone's business but ours."

That said, they'd never discussed any kind of a relationship between them, so it wasn't even *their* business.

Yet.

Butterflies took flight in her stomach as she continued to meet Sharpe's beautiful blue-eyed gaze. She waited for him to say something, to indicate whether or not anything was happening between them, but he said nothing, and after a moment his gaze dropped back to his hands on the tabletop.

She took the out he was giving her and grabbed her salad plate. "I'm going to visit the salad bar. I'll be back in a moment."

Sally's salad bar really was well stocked with a variety of items, and by the time Emma returned to the table, the moment with Sharpe had most definitely passed. Frost was now onstage, playing soft acoustic guitar in the background. Sally had returned with their sodas and pizzas, and Aidan had slipped into the booth next to Sharpe.

"What did you do in the arcade?" Sharpe asked, grabbing a slice of pizza and taking a large bite.

"They have some really cool old-school pinball machines in there," Aidan exclaimed before taking a big bite of his own pizza. What was with guys cramming as much food into their mouths at a time as they could?

Chewing with his mouth full, he said, "I'm a pinball wizard. I even made the siren and the red light on top go off."

"Wow. That's impressive," Emma said, pouring blue cheese dressing onto her lettuce. "I've never been any good at pinball. I always hit the buttons a second too late. I do the same thing when I try to hit the ball in softball. I miss every time."

"I'll have to teach you how to do it right," Sharpe said. "It's all in the technique and the timing. You'll be a pro on the church softball team before you know it."

Emma stared at him, trying to decide if there was an underlying message to what he was saying or if he was just making small talk. Church softball was played in the spring, wasn't it? And they'd be long gone by then...

Unless they wouldn't be.

She was so confused. Was he saying he wanted her to stay?

And what would she do if she did? Try to find a job that would give her enough money for Nan, Aidan and her to live on, save for the future, and provide all the benefits they needed?

For a moment she allowed her mind to

think about her dream of opening a business of her own. She'd intended to keep saving toward being a business owner for another five to ten years, but that was all before Aidan had come into her life. She owed it to her brother to do what was best for him, though she wasn't even sure what that was, exactly. Even if she had the money to open a business, what could she do in a small mountain town like Whispering Pines? What did a town like this even need that it didn't already have?

The three of them kept up small talk while they ate, although it was mostly Aidan chattering about this and that. Emma appeared oddly inattentive to the conversation, staring off into space and often looking lost in thought. Sometimes he had to repeat questions to her, and her answers were brusque or only one word.

Had Sally's teasing gotten to her? Was she only being kind in saying it didn't bother her that some of the people here thought they might be a couple?

If it bothered her, then it definitely bothered him, because more and more, he was beginning to feel as if that was something they ought to pursue. It was hardly practical, since she was leaving, and long-distance relationships rarely worked out well. Even if she visited her nan once in a while, it wouldn't be enough.

Was there some way he could convince her to stay in town? He really didn't have a lot up his sleeve to tempt her with. For all the good he saw in mountain living, he knew it wasn't for everyone, and although Emma had relaxed and become more casual over the past few weeks, she'd arrived here as a fashionable city girl, and he knew that was in her blood.

"Who's in the mood for dessert? I'm thinking of taking a trip to the ice cream parlor," came Gramps's gravelly voice as he and Emma's nan approached the table. "And before you answer, I'm only asking those who are under five feet tall here."

Sharpe raised his eyebrows. He was clearly being cut, and Emma was at least five-two, which left her out.

"It's a good thing I filled up on my salad, then, isn't it?" Emma asked with amusement. She didn't look taken aback at all. "I couldn't eat another bite."

"I'm still hungry, especially for ice cream,"

Aidan said enthusiastically. "And you guys aren't supposed to come with us, anyway. Gramps and Nan are taking me, and you have to walk Emma back to Nan's house, Sharpe."

"Shh!" Nan said, holding her forefinger over her smiling lips. "Don't give our plan away to them."

"Your *what*?" Sharpe demanded.

"Nothing, nothing," Nan insisted. "Now, we're going to take the boy out for ice cream, and you two are going to walk back to my house. Slowly. *Meander* may be the word I'm looking for. Give yourselves plenty of time to talk."

"Talk about what?" Sharpe asked. Nan had given them pretty clear directions up to this point. She might as well finish by giving them the entire script she expected them to follow.

"Son, if you can't figure that part out, you're more hopeless than I thought," Gramps said with a snort. "Use that noggin of yours."

"Never mind your noggin," Emma's nan said, shaking her head. She put her palm on Sharpe's chest, over his heart. "Think from here."

Sharpe chuckled—until he noticed how

wide-eyed Emma looked. Stunned, like the proverbial deer caught in headlights.

Not good.

"I have my truck here," he said, trying to reassure her. "I know it's a little chilly outside. I'll be happy to drive you back to your nan's, if you want."

"You will absolutely not do that," Gramps said. "If Natalie and I can brave the weather, so can the two of you."

"I don't mind walking," Emma said.

That was apparently good enough for Gramps and Nan. They took off with Aidan bouncing between them, leaving Sharpe and Emma to walk home alone.

"Well, what do you think?" he asked as he wrapped her coat around her.

"About what?" she asked, zipping her puffer jacket and adjusting the hood around her head before pulling on her white knit gloves.

"About being set up. No question that was what just happened."

"No question whatsoever. You'd have to be blind not to notice. Although I do wonder why they thought they needed to do that."

"Because as they said, they're hoping I'll

do something smart for once in my life—like maybe ask you out on a real date?"

"Could be. Clearly, we're moving too slow for them," Emma replied. "Which really doesn't make sense, because at this point, dating would be moving too fast, since I'm leaving in two weeks. Wouldn't you think?"

"Everybody has an opinion," Sharpe said with a groan. "But I gotta say, feeling as if I'm not keeping up with my eighty-year-old grandfather does make me feel a bit like I'm losing a game of chess."

"I never understood the game of chess," she said. "Or softball. So I may take you up on your offer to teach me sometime."

"Really?" His heart skipped a beat. "You'd let me teach you?"

"Depends on how good you are."

They waved to the family, and he held the door for her as they made their way outside. There was a definite nip to the air, but it wasn't too chilly. Still, as he gestured her down the street, he moved to the outside of the sidewalk and wrapped his arm around her shoulders to offer what warmth he had.

They were quiet for a minute while Sharpe

tried to figure out how to ask what his heart was burning to know.

"So…are you trying to tell me you've considered staying in Whispering Pines?" he finally asked, holding his breath as he waited for her answer.

She stopped and turned to him, her hand on his waist. He wrapped his other arm around her, so they were standing face-to-face.

"The short answer is yes. I've considered it. I'm still considering it. As far as Aidan is concerned, I know he would be all for staying here in town and growing up a country boy. And my nan would like us to stay close by. Those are on the pro list, among other things."

"The schools are great here," Sharpe was quick to point out. "Most of the teachers have been teaching since I was a kid."

"That's great to know, and it's one of the major questions I'd need answered before I made any kind of permanent decision. But there's a lot more to it than that, and it would be a huge commitment for me to make. I just don't see how it can realistically happen, as much as I'd like for it to work out."

"Like what?"

"A job, for starters."

He was opening his mouth to offer her a job at Winslow's Woodlands on the spot until her next words stopped him short.

"I not only need a salary that is at least close to what I'm making in California, but I need a strong benefit package. Everything from health, dental and vision to short-and long-term disability and a 401(k) plan. I'm not sure how many places around here offer those kinds of benefits, but I feel like I need to have those in place for Aidan, if nothing else. It's possible I could get by on a slightly smaller salary, since the cost of living is lower here, but I can't compromise on the benefits."

She was right about that. It would be difficult for her to find a job that had a full range of family benefits, never mind a salary that would even come close to matching what she was making in California. There weren't that many job openings in Whispering Pines to begin with, and most were small businesses like his and didn't offer any benefits at all, or at best the very minimum in medical benefits.

There were ways around some of those issues, of course. He'd always bought his own personal insurances, but then again, he was as healthy as a horse and didn't have anyone dependent on him.

"If you stayed through Christmas, you'd be amazed at the changes here in town," he said, trying to think of other ways Whispering Pines would make her happy. He gestured up and down the thoroughfare. "The main street's lamplights will be wrapped in tinsel and twinkling with red and green bulbs, and shopkeepers go all out on decorating their storefronts for the holidays."

"I do love Christmas lights," she agreed, though her gaze looked distant.

"We do up Winslow's Woodlands, as well, since Christmas is our busiest time of year."

"I can imagine."

Why didn't he think he was quite getting through to her?

"There's something else." She sounded so serious it made Sharpe's muscles tense from head to toe.

He reached up to brush a stray lock of auburn hair behind her ear and met her eyes. "What is it?"

"Can we walk?" She turned and held out her gloved hand to him.

"Sure." He linked his fingers with hers, and they started back down the street.

"Promise you won't laugh."

She sounded far too serious for this to be something amusing, but he nodded anyway and gestured for her to speak.

"I've always dreamed about starting my own business," she blurted out. Her pace increased, and she wouldn't look at him.

"Wait. Wait," he said, pulling back on her hand. He hadn't known exactly what she'd been about to say, but that wasn't it at all. He'd thought it would be something bad, not something wonderful. "I don't get it. Why do you think I would laugh at you? Starting your own business is a great idea, and you'd be a fantastic business owner."

"You really think so?" She looked at him then. Her eyes were glowing, and her cheeks were pinker even than they would be given the nip in the air.

"Of course. And let me be the first to tell you Whispering Pines is a great place to own a small business. The town is business-friendly, and we have a local club to support each other."

She let out a long breath. "I've never told

anyone this before," she admitted. "The only friends I have in LA are work friends, and I didn't want to jeopardize my job with news possibly getting back to my employer of me wanting to run off to chase a dream."

"You don't have any friends at church you could talk to?"

"Not really. I was working so hard to advance in my company that I didn't have time for social activities. Worship on Sunday mornings was about as much as I could manage."

"That's tough."

"So it was just something I fostered in my heart. But then, after I found out about Aidan, it felt more like a pipe dream than ever. I need to have a stable job for his sake. And if I stay here in Whispering Pines, I'll also be responsible for Nan. Which I don't mind at all. It would be good for her to have a caretaker living with her, and even better for it to be family. Of course, she'd never agree to that if she had even the slightest suspicion that's what I was doing."

Sharpe chuckled. "No, I don't imagine she would."

"Anyway..." Emma paused and let out a quiet sigh.

"What kind of business do you want to open? Something in marketing?" His mind spun trying to come up with ideas as to how Emma could use her marketing degree in Whispering Pines. Nothing immediately came to mind, however.

"I've thought about it a lot, because I'll be involved in whatever business I choose 24/7. It has to be something I love and not just business for business's sake. The job I enjoyed most over the years is when I was a barista at the college café when I was a freshman. It felt like more than just a job. I really enjoyed serving the customers and putting smiles on their faces, not to mention learning how to make good—"

"Coffee!" Sharpe exclaimed, cutting her off. "Of course. You're the Coffee Lady."

She chuckled. "Yes, I suppose you could say I am. Or at least the veterans at Mongoose's shelter seem to think so."

"It's perfect, Emma." He was getting more revved up about the idea by the second. "We don't have a café in Whispering Pines, but we could definitely use one. And all those small-business people I told you about? They'd all be your customers."

"Whoa, there. Pull back on the reins, cowboy. All this sounds wonderful, but it isn't my reality. I had planned to keep working extra hours for another five to ten years and save my money. Now I've got to take care of Aidan, and that means time and money."

"What about taking out a business loan or finding angel investors?" he asked. "I still think it's a wonderful idea."

"For a small-town café? Finding investors would be difficult. And after all I've done to get through college without debt, I'm not willing to put myself into thousands of dollars of debt now, not even to pursue my dream."

Sharpe's energy plummeted. He understood her reasoning, but it was hard for him to hear when he wanted her to stay so badly. Suddenly he had a thought. "You know what? We need to be walking the other way."

"We do?"

"Yes, we do. Come on. Let's cross the street."

Instead of walking toward her nan's house just outside town limits, he led her the other direction, and they stopped at a four-way stop sign near the middle of town.

"Close your eyes," he said, putting his

palm over her eyelids to make sure she wasn't peeking. Then he wrapped his arm around her shoulders and turned her around so she was facing an empty storefront.

"Should I be concerned?" she asked with a squeak in her voice.

"I've got you," he assured her. "Ready? Open your eyes!"

Her gaze widened the moment she laid eyes on the glass storefront with a gold-and-white-striped awning draped across the front. She didn't speak for the longest time, and he worried the shop wasn't close to what she'd been envisioning.

"This space has been sitting empty for six months," he said. "So you could probably get a really good deal on it. It used to be a barbershop, but old Mac retired, and the beauty salon down the street took on all his clients."

She still didn't say anything, just stepped forward and cupped her hands against the glass so she could peek inside.

"Not quite what you're looking for?" he asked, feeling extraordinarily disappointed. It wasn't as if this space would be the only choice if she decided to stay—and the way she was talking, she had no intention of staying—but it had popped into his head so fast he'd just thought maybe it was a God thing.

She turned, leaning her shoulders against the door of the shop, and he could see tears glimmering in her eyes.

Oh, wow.

Okay, so it wasn't perfect, but he hadn't meant to make her cry.

"I'm sorry. I just thought—"

She stepped in front of him and put her finger over his lips to stop him from speaking.

"Shh," she whispered. "Do not even think about apologizing for this. It's perfect, Sharpe. Better than I could ever have imagined. I only wish it could be real. I need time to think about it and pray about it, but if I were going to make an outrageous leap of faith, this adorable little shop here would be the very first step."

"To opening the Coffee Lady?"

"I'm crazy to even think about it, aren't I?"

"I'm crazy about you," he murmured in response.

She gasped, and he wondered if he maybe should have kept his mouth shut. It wouldn't be the first time he'd said the wrong thing. But a moment later, she framed his face with her hands, pulling his head down until her soft lips met his.

His heart raced, and his mind whirled. He hadn't even realized how much he'd wanted this moment to happen until her lips had touched his. Now he couldn't imagine that there was anything better in this world.

Forget reality. How could she even think about leaving when there was this chemistry between them that he couldn't even begin to explain?

Could she feel his support, know he'd be right by her side if she took that leap of faith?

"You're amazing," he said. "I believe in you, Coffee Lady."

Chapter Ten

❧

Coffee Lady.

Somehow Sharpe's words felt perfect—romantic and wonderful and complete.

God was so good. Sharpe believed in her. He believed in her dreams and had, for at least that one moment, helped her make them feel real.

As real as the feel of his kiss and the strength of his arms around her, drawing her near. Any chill she might have felt earlier was gone now, replaced by warmth growing and spreading throughout her with every beat of her heart.

She hadn't even realized she'd been waiting for this moment, but now that it was here, she suddenly wanted to fight for it with all her might. It might be more difficult to stay here and open a business than it would be to return to a job she disliked just because it paid well. Money was going to be an issue, and it scared her to death to consider taking on a loan she had no idea if she'd be able to repay.

On the other hand, she would be doing something she loved, something worth putting her whole heart into. And if their kiss was anything to go by, she would be building her dream with someone she deeply cared for by her side.

Sharpe pulled her into his arms, turning her so her back was against his chest and she could see the store in front of her.

"Start dreaming tonight," he whispered into her ear. "What kind of logo will you have on the front window? I'm picturing a steaming mug of coffee."

"This is still too new to me," she admitted. "I don't know how to make a dream into reality."

He pulled her even tighter. "You don't need to make any decisions tonight, other than knowing that you'd like to stay in Whispering Pines. To stay with *me*."

She turned back into his arms and gazed up at him. "That's the easiest part of imagining my future," she said, enjoying the sensation of running a palm over the scruff on his cheek. "The *best* part."

"For me, too," he murmured, leaning down to kiss her once again.

They embraced for a few more minutes until Emma shivered from the cold. As nice as it was to be in Sharpe's arms, the temperature was dropping fast.

"Let's get you home," he suggested. "I'll drive you."

They returned to Sally's Pizza, and Sharpe revved up the engine. They sat for a few minutes talking quietly as the heater warmed the cab.

He held her hand the entire drive home. She couldn't stop looking at him. Her heart was singing that she'd finally found a man who was worth taking a risk for. Until they parted tonight, she wasn't going to let reality have its say.

When they arrived at her house, there was a moment of awkward pause before Sharpe reached across the cab and brushed his lips lightly across hers.

"When are we going to let everyone know they were right about us?" he asked.

His question immediately pulled back the reins on her emotions. They couldn't just suddenly be a couple, even if they wanted to be. They had to tread carefully.

They were both avoiding the truth, and they knew it. It was one thing to talk about hopes and dreams, but as much as she wanted it, they would only be a couple for as long as she stayed in town.

"If we're going to be in any kind of relationship, I think we need to sit down with Aidan first and ask him how he feels about it," she suggested.

He grinned. "You're right, but I think I already know the answer to that question. After all, he was part of the setup tonight."

"I know. And I think he'll be over the moon if you'll keep mentoring him."

"Of course I will. I wouldn't have it any other way."

"What about the other thing?" she asked tentatively, her heart doing a little flip.

"The...*other* thing?"

"He thinks the sun rises and sets because of you, so I have no doubt he will think I'm making a good choice in who I'm dating, but I'm not so sure he'll think I'm good enough for you."

"Then he has it backward." He took her hand and kissed the back of it. "I'm excited to see where this goes between us. And I'm also pumped at the thought of getting a coffee shop in town. You'll have lines going around the corner."

"Please don't push me, Sharpe. I can't just make unilateral decisions without praying through it. It's still not any kind of reality for me."

He chuckled. "No. I'm the one who makes *those* kinds of decisions. I see things in black and white, and I just go and do what I think needs to be done. There have definitely been times in my life when it's hurt me not to think things through better."

"Like what?"

"I thought I was trapped here at Winslow's Woodlands, chained in by my responsibilities to my family and the farm. While that was somewhat true, I now recognize that the grass isn't always greener on the other side. Just because I couldn't leave doesn't mean I should have if I'd had the opportunity to do so. And now more than ever, I don't want to. I'm happy exactly where I am."

"I'm glad to hear it, because I'm happy

you're here, too. My stay in Whispering Pines wouldn't have been nearly as interesting without you."

She didn't want to say good-night, but they couldn't linger forever, so she leaned over and gave him one last kiss before exiting the truck and rushing to the front door to get out of the bitter cold.

When she closed the door, she leaned her back against it and pressed a hand over her heart, listening as Sharpe's truck moved away.

What a night. She couldn't ever have imagined she would experience the emotions that were now whirling through her. Sharpe was an amazing man, and he was interested in her, and everything should be perfect—except it wasn't.

She thought about talking to Aidan, but when she peeked in on him, she found he was already asleep.

That was okay. They could talk tomorrow morning. In the meantime, she'd make herself a cup of hot cocoa and read in bed.

Anything to keep her mind from thinking about reality.

She'd only been reading for fifteen minutes

when her cell phone buzzed. She reached for the phone so quickly she nearly dropped it, expecting to see Sharpe's face on the screen.

It was, and her heart started hammering. She couldn't help the grin that instantly formed on her face. Was he calling to tell her he already missed her as much as she missed him, so much that he couldn't even wait until tomorrow to talk to her again?

"Hey, there," she answered, her voice getting choked up over the words. "I was just thinking about you."

She wasn't at all used to being flirtatious, but the words just seemed to slip out.

"Emma." His use of her name sounded as if he'd just dropped a huge rock into a deep gully.

What was wrong?

Had he taken the time to think about what had happened earlier and already realized it was all a big mistake?

"Sharpe?" she shot back when he didn't continue speaking. "What's going on? What happened?"

"I just got a call from St. Joseph's Hospital," Sharpe said, his voice breaking. "It's Mongoose. He's been stabbed."

* * *

Sharpe had received the call just after he'd gotten back from taking Emma home. He'd practically been floating on air, he was so happy at the way things had gone. And now there was the possibility that Emma and Aidan would be staying in town for an extended period of time—maybe forever, if he had anything to say about it.

He finally felt as if he could break down the walls that had been so carefully guarding his heart. He could tentatively start thinking with joy toward the future and not just about everything he'd had to miss by staying home and caring for his siblings and the farm.

Emma was amazing, and God was so good!

God was good *all the time*, he had to remind himself after the hospital called him. That was what Mongoose would say, no matter what situation he found himself in.

Sharpe was Tre'Monte Williams's emergency contact, and Sharpe's cell phone had started ringing about a half hour after he'd returned to the farm. He'd thought maybe it was Emma and had been confused and bummed when it was a number he didn't recognize.

When he'd discovered it was the hospital

and his friend had been hurt, he had to fore-
stall the panic rising in him. He couldn't get
much information from the nurse other than
that Mongoose had been stabbed in the shoulder but that he was conscious and stable.

As soon as Sharpe hung up the phone, he
dialed Emma. He didn't think twice about
why he reached out to Emma first, only that
he needed support and knew she'd be the one
he wanted by his side.

*Dear Lord in Heaven, please wrap
Tre'Monte in Your loving arms and keep him
safe. Let him know You're by his side. May
he feel Your presence, Lord.*

"I'll be right over," Emma told him as soon
as he'd related the horrible news about Mongoose. "You sit tight until I get there. You
won't be in any state to drive, worrying over
your friend. You said St. Joseph's."

"He went to the local urgent care, but apparently it's bad enough that he was transferred by ambulance to St. Joseph's."

"I'll be there in ten minutes."

Sharpe hung up the phone and paced the
room, scrubbing his fingers through his hair
and wondering what he should be doing. He
needed to be thinking logically, even though

his heart was practically beating out of his chest. He put his snow boots back on, as well as his wool-lined jean jacket and his cowboy hat, but there seemed to be little else for him to do to keep his mind occupied until Emma arrived.

Thankfully, Emma was as good as her word and pulled in front of the farmhouse less than ten minutes later, no makeup on and her hair tousled as if she'd been sleeping.

"Sorry if I woke you," he immediately apologized. He hadn't even considered that she may already have been asleep.

"Oh, no. I was still awake. So tell me— what happened to Mongoose? Did a fight break out in the shelter?"

"Honestly, I don't know all the details yet. I guess we'll have to ask him about that. If the nurse had any idea how he got stabbed, she wasn't exactly forthcoming, even though I'm Mongoose's emergency contact. I guess because I'm not immediate family, they're keeping closemouthed about it. Or maybe they don't know what happened. It would be just like Mongoose to be tight-lipped about a fight."

He was angry that he didn't know more, but he supposed it didn't make a difference except that he would have been even more worried if he'd gotten specifics. He could only get there as fast as he could get there. This way he could see how Mongoose was with his own eyes.

They didn't speak much on the hour ride down to St. Joseph's, each lost in their own thoughts. Sharpe was imagining all the different ways Mongoose could have gotten in that kind of trouble, but he knew his friend would set the record straight soon enough.

Stabbed, though.

How could that even happen to a Delta Force operative? Sharpe couldn't even imagine a scenario where a man with a knife would get the best of his friend.

When they reached the hospital, they went straight upstairs to his room, which had been the only useful information Sharpe had been able to coax from the otherwise closemouthed nurse.

While Emma hung back, Sharpe swept his cowboy hat off, knocked on the door and stuck his head in.

"I know they just brought you in not too long ago," he said to Mongoose. "Are you up to seeing a couple of visitors?"

Mongoose actually chuckled. "Please. There's nothing on TV, and I'm already bored out of my skull."

"Now, that's exactly what a man who has spent his life chasing adrenaline would say. What happened, buddy?" he asked gently, pulling up a chair next to his friend, whose arm was in a sling. He had an IV in his other arm, which Mongoose explained was flooding antibiotics into his system because they hadn't picked up the knife that had stabbed him, so they didn't have any idea how dirty it was.

"I also had to have a tetanus shot," he growled, though he flashed Emma a toothy grin as she entered the room and moved to the other side of the bed. "That hurt worse than the wound itself."

He paused and winked at Emma. "I didn't realize I'd have to go and get stabbed to get to see the pretty Coffee Lady again. I would have gotten myself stabbed last week."

"I'm sorry I haven't been back again to visit the shelter," Emma said. "Things have been…busy. I probably won't be in town more than another week, and then I'll be headed back to my job in California."

Sharpe noticed she didn't say her *home* in California, but rather her *job*. Oddly, it gave him a sense of hope.

"Well, if you stay," said Mongoose, "I hope you'll come back to volunteer at the shelter every once in a while. The men really appreciated you and Aidan."

"Says the man who just got stabbed," Sharpe pointed out. "And you want to put her in the same situation?"

Sharpe appreciated everything Mongoose did more than he could say, but the man was former Delta Force. He shouldn't be thinking of putting Emma and Aidan into harm's way, even for the good of the veterans. Sharpe knew he was being overprotective, and it was Emma's decision to make, but he couldn't help wanting to keep her and Aidan safe.

"Help me sit this bed up a little, and I'll tell you all about what happened."

Emma found the bed controls and slowly moved him to a sitting position. He grimaced, and she immediately stopped.

"I'm sorry. I didn't mean to hurt you. Can I get the nurse to get you something for the pain?"

Mongoose frowned and shook his head. "This ain't that bad compared to some situations I've been in," he said, gesturing to his bandaged shoulder. "And after all I've seen down at the shelter, I told the nurse I just wanted plain ol' Tylenol and that's all. That way I have nothing to hide when the boys ask about it—which some of them will."

Admiration flashed through Emma's eyes, and Sharpe had to admit he was pretty impressed, as well. That wound had to hurt, yet Mongoose was always thinking of his men first. That was what had made him such a good leader both in the army and at the homeless shelter.

"So, what happened?" Emma asked softly. "How did you get stabbed? Was there a fight at the shelter?"

Mongoose shook his head and then clamped his jaw against the pain. He might be a martyr for the sake of his men, but he was still hurting.

"It had nothing to do with the veterans," Mongoose assured her. "I run a tight ship. What happened tonight was there was an argument going on right outside my shelter where all the men could see."

"Gang members?" Sharpe asked, his brow furrowing.

"Honestly? I don't know. All I know for certain is that there were four young men on each side facing off, and they all had weapons—guns and knives and who knows what else. I can't have a fight like that right outside my shelter. It could send any one of my guys into a bad place in a second. So I went outside to see if I could talk them down."

"That obviously went well," Sharpe said dryly, tucking his hands into the front pockets of his jeans. Emma looked as if she wanted to pelt him with something, and he shrugged.

Mongoose chuckled. "Eight to one are good odds for a man like me, so I didn't think twice about meddling in their affairs. It was the ninth guy who bolted around the corner at the last minute and jabbed me in the shoulder with his butterfly knife that got me. I should have seen him coming. I'm getting rusty in my old age. Still, I stopped the fight, right?"

"Yes, but at what cost?" Emma demanded, laying a comforting hand on his arm.

"It's nothing. Really. It's a clean wound, straight in and out of my shoulder muscle. Trust me. I've had much worse injuries during my time, including bullets and shrapnel. This little wound is small in comparison. I'll be going home in a couple of days, just as soon as they finish with these antibiotics and are convinced I'm on the mend."

"Is it okay if we bring Aidan over with us tomorrow?" Sharpe asked, half to Mongoose and half to Emma.

"Do you think that's a good idea?" Emma asked, her gaze widening.

Mongoose was already nodding.

"It's a good life lesson for Aidan," Sharpe explained. "And I want him to bring Baloo with him so he can discover yet another way he's useful as a service dog."

"He can make veterans smile, and apparently people in the hospital, as well. He can herd sheep. And let's not forget the country dancing. What else can that dog do?" Emma said, shaking her head in amazement.

Sharpe grinned but didn't speak aloud.

He can be a boy's best friend.

Chapter Eleven

Emma knew Aidan was always happy to go somewhere with Baloo, even someplace scary like a hospital. The boy had really come out of his shell over the past few weeks, and as long as Sharpe and Baloo were there, the idea of going to visit a sick person didn't really seem to bother him.

That the person in question was Mongoose probably had something to do with it, Emma supposed. Aidan really liked Mongoose, and he didn't balk for a second when Sharpe had suggested they go visit him. Emma was concerned Aidan might think it was cool that Mongoose had been stabbed, but maybe seeing the real thing would give him a perspective he wouldn't otherwise have.

Emma knew Sharpe was in much better

emotional shape today than he'd been last night, and he'd offered to drive the truck, especially since they were taking the dog with them. Emma was getting used to Baloo going wherever Aidan went, and she wondered what would happen when they had to leave him behind. It would break her brother's heart, and that would break Emma's.

Yet one more tick in the *stay* box she was mentally putting together. For Aidan, leaving Baloo would be a real trial.

Aidan didn't have to be told how to put on Baloo's service dog vest anymore. It had become second nature to him. Sharpe gave him instructions as they entered the hospital and stopped at the front desk to register Baloo. Evidently it wasn't the first time the border collie had visited St. Joseph's as a therapy dog, and the people at the desk knew him well.

"When we get into Mongoose's room, bring Baloo alongside the bed so Mongoose can pet him with his good arm, okay?"

Aidan nodded.

"That's a lot of what you have to do when you bring in a therapy dog, especially to a hospital," Sharpe continued. "Try to figure out what's the best way for the patient to be able to reach out and interact with Baloo. The dog is pretty smart about these things, too, and has a natural instinct, so trust him. But at the end of the day, he will respond to your commands, so try to think like the patient."

"Is he allowed to jump on the bed?" Aidan queried, which Emma thought was an exceptionally thoughtful question.

"If the patient asks and Baloo can jump up without getting in the way of any medical tubes or IVs, then yes, it's okay. Again, use your best judgment. A lot of the kids in the children's ward like to have Baloo up on the bed with them."

"Hey, there, Mongoose," Sharpe called as they entered his room. The big man was up and sitting in a chair now, staring out the window and looking thoroughly bored. He brightened right up when they entered, especially when he saw Aidan and Baloo.

"Who've you brought for me today?" Mongoose asked, smiling at Aidan.

"Baloo. He's here to make you feel better, Mongoose."

"Well, he is certainly doing that," he said as Aidan brought Baloo to Mongoose's side. "And I'm glad to see you here, too."

"Sharpe said Baloo helps patients in the hospital feel better," Aidan explained with a grin. "Dogs always make people happy."

"That's a fact," Mongoose agreed, scrubbing Baloo between his ears.

Emma was proud of Aidan, and she was impressed that Sharpe didn't try to make all the calls for the boy. He was allowing her brother to take charge.

"And I think it's really awesome that you like to help people, Aidan. I hope you'll be able to come back to the shelter someday," Mongoose continued.

"I…uh…" Aidan stammered, and then his face fell. Emma didn't have to ask why. Nor did she need Aidan to verbalize how he felt about staying in Whispering Pines. It was in every move he made, every expression, every gesture.

"And you, Emma," Mongoose continued with a wink.

Sharpe shuffled from boot to boot and crossed his arms. He looked so uncomfortable with Mongoose's easy manner that Emma wanted to giggle.

Sharpe cares for me.

And that made all the difference in the world. It was amazing how one night could change everything. She'd told Sharpe she needed to pray about her answer as to whether to leave or stay, and she did. She wasn't about to make a hasty decision about something as critical as doing a good job as Aidan's big sister and guardian. But with every moment that passed, she became more and more aware of all Whispering Pines and Sharpe Winslow had to offer her.

Mentoring Aidan, for one. Showing him how to help people, both at the hospital and at the veterans' shelter. Learning new skills he'd be able to use for the rest of his life.

And that was nothing to say of the kiss she and Sharpe had shared. Talk about life-changing. She had a reason. If only God would show her a path to stay, open her eyes to a solution she hadn't yet thought of.

"They're cutting me loose this afternoon," Mongoose told them. "I think I'm bothering them too much, so they just want to get rid of me as soon as possible." He laughed. "Can I help it if I'm used to being active and am bored to tears stuck in this chair?"

Emma didn't believe for a second that Mongoose would be rude to anyone, nurses or otherwise, but she let him crow on about it. He needed an outlet for all the energy he couldn't otherwise expend right now.

"But you got stabbed?" Aidan said, sounding fascinated in the way only a preteen boy could do.

Mongoose looked him right in the eye. "I was breaking up a fight that shouldn't have been happening at all. You've got to promise me you won't go getting into fights, Aidan. Real men are better than that."

Aidan's gaze widened, but he immediately nodded. "Yes, sir."

"Good, then," Mongoose said, patting Aidan's shoulder.

"Well, since you'll be leaving soon," Sharpe said, "I think, if you don't mind, we'll get out of here and take Aidan around the ward to cheer up people who really need the cheering up. Not ones who are going to be perpetually grouchy no matter how many dogs they get to see," Sharpe teased.

"Ha. Don't let the door hit you on your way out."

Sharpe grunted and jammed his hat on his head. "You've gotta wonder why I'm his emergency contact," he mumbled under his breath. "I'm the last person he wants around when he's laid up."

Emma put her hand on Sharpe's arm. "That's not true, and you know it. He was just trying to be kind to Aidan."

"Yeah, I know. Let's go to the nurses' desk and find out who's up for a therapy dog visit today."

Before they even got the list of names and door numbers, Aidan was surrounded by a gaggle of nurses, both male and female, who were ecstatic over having a dog on the floor. Baloo loved the attention, as did Aidan. And he did a great job directing the dog around, interacting with the patients and leaving everyone with a smile.

"So…about Thanksgiving," Sharpe said as they exited the hospital and loaded Baloo and Aidan back into the truck.

"Yeah. That's right. What time do you want us over? It's really kind of you to invite us to spend the holiday with your family. We can't wait."

"As if Gramps would have it any other way. He and your grandmother are connected at the hip these days."

Emma grinned. "They are. And I couldn't be happier for them."

"He's not the only one who wants your family there, though," Sharpe said, a half smile curling up one side of his lip. "It wouldn't be the same without you. I've kinda gotten used to having you around."

"Back atcha," she said, her throat suddenly becoming dry and gravelly.

"But that wasn't what I wanted to talk about. You can count on the best turkey and fixings you've ever tasted, compliments of Jake and Avery, but before we do our big sit-down dinner at the bed-and-breakfast, the Winslow family has another holiday tradition I expect you'll like to take advantage of."

"Yes? And what's that?"

"We go as a family to serve Thanksgiving dinner to the men at Mongoose's shelter."

"Really?" Her whole countenance jumped with excitement, and adrenaline coursed through her. She'd get to be the Coffee Lady again, and she couldn't wait.

"I'm sure Mongoose will be thrilled to see you there," Sharpe said blithely, his fist tightening on the wheel.

He had to know how she felt about him, but she suspected he was just trying to get her to admit it aloud.

"That'll be nice," she said and then paused, teasing him a little. "But you know who I'm most interested in standing next to as I serve the men?"

"No. Who would that be?"

She reached across the cab and threaded her fingers through his. "There's this cowboy who once came and saved my younger brother from getting into a fight," she said with a tender smile. "At the time I thought he was a little bit intimidating. But now that I've gotten to know him better, I can't help but want to spend more time with him. If that's what he wants, too," she added, glancing his direction.

He wore a full-on smile now, his eyes gleaming with happiness.

"That cowboy," he replied, "can't wait to spend Thanksgiving with you and your brother. I know you're praying for direction for your lives. I'm praying that you'll find direction, as well—right into my arms."

The Winslows had been serving Thanksgiving dinner at the homeless shelter for several years now, ever since Sharpe had first met Mongoose. This year was no different, except for the addition of Emma and Aidan and their nan to the group. That, and the fact that Mongoose was left directing traffic in a sling he had to wear for several more weeks.

Without being told, Aidan worked his way around the room with Baloo by his side. The boy was every bit as natural and instinctual as the dog. Sharpe loved how much Aidan had come out of his shell in the weeks since he'd first come to town. The truth was, Baloo didn't belong to Sharpe anymore. Whether or not the Fitzpatricks stayed in Whispering Pines, Baloo ought to be with Aidan. It was yet one more thing he wanted to talk over with Emma when the time was right.

But that all hinged on her big decision, and he'd decided not to push her on it for fear it would drive her away from the town—and, more importantly, from him. Trying to push a dog on her when she was considering going back to a city apartment might be too much. As hard as it was, he had to give her space to work it out between herself and God. But it couldn't hurt to put in a little prayer intention of his own.

Mongoose called for lunch and a prayer, bowing his head and saying grace in a low, fervent bass voice. Aidan took his place behind the roll steamer just as he'd done the last time he was here. Sharpe stood next to him, peeking under the lid to find a delicious-smelling green bean casserole. He was going to be hungry by the time they got back home for their own Thanksgiving meal. Jake was an amazing cook and had taken full charge of the holiday meal since he'd married Avery and they'd started their bed-and-breakfast together.

For a moment, Sharpe looked around and couldn't find Emma, but then he spotted her in the back corner with the coffee carafe in her hand, smiling and chatting up a small group of veterans as she refilled their cups. Was it possible she was imagining her own café, one with *The Coffee Lady* printed on the window out front?

He certainly was.

Everyone she spoke to smiled as she gave each of them her full attention. She was happy to take thermoses from the men and fill them with fresh, hot coffee from the machine. She was buzzing around like a bee.

Their time at the shelter went by in a blink, and before Sharpe knew it, they were all loaded up and back in Whispering Pines. Emma, Aidan and Baloo were with him in his truck, and other family members were driving together in other vehicles. He wasn't certain who'd taken Gramps and Emma's nan, but he wasn't worried that they'd somehow managed to catch a ride.

He'd hoped Emma would say something on the way home regarding her decision of whether or not to stay in town, but she was unusually quiet, staring out the passenger window at the scenery. He reached for her hand, and she accepted his gesture, but it wasn't even enough to get her to turn toward him.

He glanced back to make sure Aidan had his earbuds in, which, as usual, he did, his head resting on the seat and his eyes closed. The only way Sharpe knew he was still awake was that he was stroking Baloo's fur, but hopefully his music was playing loud enough that he wouldn't hear any conversation coming from the front seat.

"A penny for your thoughts?" he asked Emma in a whisper.

"Hmm?" She glanced over at him, looking dazed.

"You seemed distant just now."

She shook her head and then glanced back at Aidan as Sharpe had done.

"No. Just lost in thought."

"About?"

"We're going to be leaving on Saturday."

"What? You've made your final decision?" Sharpe's heart plummeted into his gut, where it lodged like a rock.

"I just don't see any other way around it. As much as I would love to stay here and pursue my dream, it just isn't practical. Whispering Pines has been like a daydream, and I've loved every second of it, as has Aidan. But it can't stay that way forever. As it is, I've put off making a decision so long that we're going to have to stay in a hotel until I can find more permanent lodgings for us. Hopefully something near the building where I work." She blew out a breath and scrubbed a hand down her face.

Sharpe forced a ragged breath into his lungs. He felt like falling apart, but doing that would hurt Emma, and he'd never do that to her, so he tamped down his feelings. He knew she hadn't made this decision to leave lightly. He could hear the pain in her voice.

"I understand," he said, his voice gravelly with emotion.

Her grip tightened around his hand.

Sharpe cleared his throat. "I don't want to make this any harder for you than it already is, but since you'll be looking for a new apartment anyway, would it be possible to find one that would accept a medium-size border collie?"

Tears sprang to her eyes and poured down her cheeks, and she rushed to wipe them off before Aidan saw.

"But he's your dog," she said quietly.

Sharpe chuckled despite the pain in his gut. "You really think so? He hasn't been my dog for a while now. This move is going to be rough on Aidan. I thought I could make it a little easier for him if I gifted Baloo to him, so he wouldn't be going off to California without a friend."

"Oh, Sharpe. You're so thoughtful. I'd be a fool not to accept such a kind gift on Aidan's behalf. I'll figure something out. There are places that accept dogs."

He jerked a short nod. "Good, then. It's settled."

"There's one more thing I want to ask you," she said. "I thought tomorrow, being our last full day here, we could maybe do something special together, just the three of us. Plus, I have an idea that will make Nan happy."

"Sure. What did you have in mind?" There was no question that he was going to spend her final day here with her. How could he not?

"Would you give us the full Christmas tree–cutting experience? I thought we could get one for Nan's house. What do you think?"

"I think that's a wonderful idea." He glanced back to make sure the boy wasn't listening, but he was rocking out to his tunes, his hands moving as if he were playing the drums. "I'll tell Aidan about Baloo then. Make an early Christmas present of him."

"Trust me when I say that will be the very best gift he's ever had." She sniffled but had stemmed her tears. "It will mean so much to him. And to me."

He brushed his thumb across the top of her hand. "And to me, as well. We'll make tomorrow the best day ever, something we'll remember all of our lives, okay?"

He would remember it, all right, for as long as he lived—as the biggest heartbreak of his life, and one from which he didn't know if he would ever recover. After all these years fighting the feeling of being stuck where he was, he'd think he would be over the worst of it.

But the worst was yet to come.

Chapter Twelve

Despite having shed tears earlier in Sharpe's truck, Emma couldn't help but smile as she sat at the Winslow family dinner table—dinner *tables*, really, because there was no way to seat that many people around a single table. The bed-and-breakfast was equipped to handle a number of people at a time, so the adults sat around a long row of tables that had been pushed together. The older children sat together at another table. Of all the adults, it surprised her that Frost was the one who volunteered his services for the children's table. He appeared to be a natural with them—the fun uncle.

It was so nice to have extended family around. She and Aidan were both going to miss times like this.

Gramps was sitting at the head of the table with Nan by his side. Avery had made calligraphy seating cards between each two place settings, indicating which couple belonged where. It made Emma's heart skip when she saw her name underneath Sharpe's. This would be the last time they would be considered a couple, and she was determined to enjoy it, no matter how brokenhearted she felt on the inside.

With Saturday practically staring her in the face, she knew she had to make the announcement that she and Aidan were leaving soon, but she'd talked it over with Sharpe before they'd come in and she'd decided to let everyone know after her Christmas tree–cutting experience tomorrow. She knew she'd see most of the siblings working at Winslow's Woodlands on the busy day after Thanksgiving, and for those she didn't see in person, the news would spread quickly via the gossip train. If she spoke out this evening during Thanksgiving dinner, it would become the major topic of conversation, and she wanted to talk about anything *but* leaving. That would ruin everything.

As Sharpe had told her at Sally's Pizza,

anywhere the Winslows were gathered became a noisy occasion where one had to talk loudly to be heard. Tonight was no different, with a number of conversations going on at once and a buzz of excitement in the air. Aidan was in an animated conversation with Frost, who was asking him about how he liked working with Baloo at the hospital and homeless shelter.

When all the food dishes had been spread on the table before them, Gramps quieted the crowd with a shrill whistle—evidently *not* a genetic trait—and asked everyone to join hands so he could say grace, especially thanking God for bringing the Fitzpatricks into their home and into their lives. The Winslows, he asserted, were better people for the new people sitting around their table. As Gramps blessed the food and ended with a hearty *amen*, Sharpe squeezed Emma's hand tightly.

The dishes were passed around, and everyone dug in. Emma noticed the noise decibel significantly decreased while everyone was focused on the food. And she had to admit Sharpe had been right when he'd praised Jake's cooking. She'd never enjoyed a meal more in her life—although that might be as much because of the company as it was the food.

Thanksgivings had never before been a thing for her. When she was young, her parents used to go out to fancy restaurants with friends on Thanksgiving and would leave her at home with a babysitter to eat a microwaved turkey meal. She'd spent her adult Thanksgivings alone and had never bothered to make a big deal out of the food she'd eaten.

"Save room for pie," Sharpe instructed her after they'd already been eating for a quarter of an hour.

"Pie?" she squeaked. "That would have been nice to know before I started. I'm feeling just as stuffed as the turkey over there."

"Find a little room in there somewhere," Sharpe said. "We have pumpkin, cherry and apple to choose from. Or you can be like me and have all three smothered in ice cream or whipped cream."

"You seriously eat all three kinds of pie? Where do you put it all?" Sharpe was a large man, but he was pure muscle from working the farm.

Avery overheard the conversation and chuckled. "Both of my brothers can put away dessert like nobody's business," she said. "And then along came our husbands, and we discovered they, too, have that raw talent. It appears to be a manly ability."

"Say what you will," Jake said, bellowing with laughter, "but Thanksgiving only comes around once a year. We all need to make the most of it."

"And we'll have leftovers," Ruby said. "For the next month, with as much food as Jake cooks. You can take some of your favorites home with you if you'd like."

Emma swallowed hard, willing back the tears that instantly sprang to her eyes. There would be no Winslow leftovers for her this year, or any year, for that matter. Sharpe reached for her arm, but she couldn't look at him, because she knew she'd break down. She took a small slice of cherry pie and ate slowly. It took her a few minutes to feel in control of her emotions again.

When everyone was finished with dessert, Gramps stood and whistled for attention again. Emma laid her hand on Sharpe's bicep and caught his gaze, mimicking Gramps's whistle and flashing him a knowing grin. He rolled his eyes.

"As you all know," Gramps began, clasping his suit jacket, "life has been difficult for me for the past couple of years. I honestly believed I'd never love again. Then God brought this special woman into my life, and she changed everything."

Gramps reached for Nan's hand and pulled her to her feet, then kissed her knuckles and grinned widely at those around the table.

"I'm long past being able to drop to one knee to do this romantically, so you'll have to bear with me and just imagine I'm kneeling and can get back up again." He reached into the inside pocket of his jacket and pulled out a sparkling ring, a large emerald surrounded by smaller diamonds. "My sweetheart was born in May, and emeralds are her birthstone," he explained.

He paused for effect and then pressed her left palm to his heart. "My love, will you make this old man feel young again and consent to be my wife?"

Nan held out her right hand, palm up. "That depends. Let me see the ring first."

Emma gaped and met Sharpe's eyes. Surely Nan wouldn't reject Gramps in front of everyone. Sharpe just grinned and shook his head.

Without hesitation, Gramps dropped the ring into her grasp. She made a big production of examining it, as if she would know by looking at it whether or not it was genuine. The entire room was silent, although Jake was smothering laughter behind his palm.

"Yes, this rings appears to have come from the heart," she said after letting Gramps sweat for a long moment. "I say, let's do this thing."

She handed him the ring back, and he tenderly placed it onto her finger, to hoots and hollers from the whole Winslow clan. All the adults swarmed around them, waiting for their turn to offer their congratulations to the happy couple.

Emma couldn't have been more delighted for Nan, nor sadder for herself. It was strange, being able to feel both emotions at the same time.

She hugged Nan and kissed Gramps on the cheek, offering her most hearty congratulations and well-wishes, and then moved out of the way so others could do the same. She was walking back to her seat when her cell phone buzzed in her pocket.

Who would be calling her on Thanksgiving Day? Everyone she knew in Whispering Pines was already here in this room.

She glanced at the screen and saw it was her attorney. Her gut tightened. Something had to be seriously wrong for him to be calling on a holiday. She excused herself and stepped outside onto the porch, wrapping one arm around her middle to stay warm.

"Hello?" she said. "Bryan? What's up? Is everything okay?"

"Hi, Emma. I hope you're having a nice Thanksgiving. I'm really sorry to have to call you today, but something has come up that I think we need to talk about in person. The sooner, the better. I'm sure you're busy celebrating right now, but is there any way you can give me a call this evening?"

"I— Yes, of course. What time?"

"Shall we say eight o'clock?"

"Okay. I'll speak to you then."

Her lawyer hung up before she'd had the opportunity to think over what he'd just said. Something had come up—something important enough they needed to speak tonight to discuss it. She'd thought her parents' whole estate had been dealt with. What if Bryan had found hidden debts? That had been one of her biggest fears from the beginning when she'd discovered she was the executor of her parents' estate. She wouldn't put it past her father to have taken out loans. He'd never been particularly good with money.

She had a bit of money set aside from selling off the items in their home at auction, but she'd intended to put that into Aidan's trust. Hopefully if her father owed anything, the money from the estate sale would cover it.

Her gut churned just thinking about it.

"Hey, there you are. I looked around and you had disappeared. Is everything okay, honey?" Sharpe stepped out the front door and closed it behind him, then moved to her side and wrapped his arm around her, offering her both comfort and warmth.

"To be honest, I don't know," she said. "I just got off a phone call from my attorney. He wants me to phone him tonight."

"On Thanksgiving? That's kind of weird, don't you think?"

"He says it's important, and that we need to speak immediately."

Sharpe stared at her for a moment without speaking before he reached out and curled a stray lock of hair behind her ear.

"That could mean it's a good thing, couldn't it?"

She took a deep breath, considering.

"I suppose. But I doubt it. It's my parents' estate we're talking about here. I thought I had it all wrapped up, paying off his debts and everything and making sure all of Aidan's money has been put in a trust for him. I have a bad feeling in my gut right now. What if my attorney has found more my dad has owed? I'm going to be really angry if I have to pay out all the money from the estate sale to settle up. That money is for Aidan's future."

Sharpe's brow lowered, and his eyes glimmered with anger on her behalf. "Is this going to hold up your plans to move back to California?"

There might have been a note of hope in Sharpe's voice, but she couldn't blame him for trying to make lemonade out of lemons.

"I don't think so. Like I said, I've worked everything out. Or at least, I thought I did. I guess I'll see tonight how bad it is."

Sharpe started to speak and then closed his mouth, choosing instead simply to wrap both arms around her and tuck her head under his chin.

Maybe it was bad news, maybe not. But

right here, right now, in the circle of Sharpe's strong arms, she felt protected.

She felt loved.

Sharpe had had a sleepless night, tossing and turning and worrying about Emma. He'd hoped she'd text or call him to let him know how it had gone with her attorney, but his phone had remained ominously silent. He thought a thousand times about reaching out to her, but she knew where he was if she wanted to talk. If she needed space, he'd give her space.

This morning, he'd dressed for the snow and had saddled three horses, his own, named Rocky, Aidan's Diamond and Emma's Elijah. Funny how he thought of Emma and Aidan whenever he saw these horses anymore. They'd be riding a short distance into the mountains to select the perfect Christmas tree for Nan. They'd cut it down and then drag it back to the farm, where Sharpe would put it in his truck and drive it to Nan's. Emma would pull out the Christmas decorations, and they'd surprise Nan with the finished product.

Sharpe also planned to tell Aidan that

Baloo was his to keep. Emma was supposed to tell Aidan they were leaving before Sharpe gave him the dog. That way the boy would have something positive to hold on to instead of just being sad that they were leaving.

Emma and Aidan arrived right on time, at ten in the morning. Both appeared surprisingly chipper, all things considered, and Sharpe wondered if she'd not yet found the voice to be able to let Aidan know they were moving away. Or maybe Aidan already knew and was okay with it. He watched the boy for a moment while he wrestled with Baloo and thought about how happy it would make him to be given the dog as a gift. Sharpe would have to find a way to pull Emma aside and ask her what had happened with the attorney, so he didn't make a muddle of things and accidentally blurt out something that was Emma's news to share.

They mounted up and headed for the hills along a trail with which Sharpe was expertly familiar, Baloo running alongside the horses and occasionally disappearing as he chased a rabbit or a squirrel. Sharpe often took families out this way to choose and cut their own trees. It was one of his favorite parts of this business. He wasn't great at interacting with people, but he did love watching the children's eyes shine at the hope and expectation of Christmas.

Aidan likewise had that gleam in his eyes. The boy loved riding Diamond, and he and Sharpe had gone on several rides, both to the pumpkin patch and along some of the many trails leading out from the farm. He probably would have given the boy the horse, as well, if he thought there was any way Aidan could keep a horse in his city apartment. The thought amused him and made him smile despite the agonizing ache in his heart.

When the trail widened and allowed, Emma drew Elijah up next to Rocky and tilted her head back, taking in the late-autumn sunshine. "It's stunning out here," she said with a contented sigh. "There's nothing else in the world like crisp mountain air."

Was she trying to bottle the memory in order to take it out later to enjoy? It was so hard for him to watch, but he would do his best to give her the time she needed.

"We should start looking for the perfect tree," he said. "What size will work best for your nan's house?"

"I measured last night after Nan was asleep," she said, mentioning nothing about returning from seeing the attorney. "I'd like to find something around six and a half feet tall. Once we put the angel on top of the tree, that'll make it about seven feet, which will be perfect to display right in front of Nan's front window."

Sharpe dismounted and tethered Rocky to a low branch. He then turned to Emma and offered her a hand down. Aidan was already dismounted by the time he looked to see how the boy was doing. He tethered the other two horses and unwrapped his chain saw, and they started walking around taking in the evergreen trees around them—pines, blue spruces and Douglas firs.

"I'm six-two, so we're looking for something about a foot taller than me."

Aidan squinted in the sunlight. "Your math is wrong," he stated bluntly.

Sharpe burst out in laughter. "Well, buddy, you'd be right about that, except we have to take into account that we're going to cut down the tree, so we'll lose some inches off the trunk. Does that make sense?"

"Oh. I get it." Aidan beamed at him before

dashing off with Baloo at his heel to look around at different trees.

Sharpe met Emma's gaze, questioning her without a word. He held his breath, and his whole body tensed as he waited for her to speak up. She opened her mouth, then pointed and exclaimed, "Look at that one. I think it's perfect!"

A tree. She was talking about a tree.

Frustration seethed through him. Did she not realize how worried he was about her? He was going to jump out of his skin if she didn't put him out of his misery soon.

"Aidan, come look at this tree." She walked all the way around the thickly branched Douglas fir, checking for any gaps and finding none. "Come on, guys. I need your opinion here. What do you think? Will Nan like it?"

Sharpe was more concerned with how *Emma* liked it, but he figured that was about the same thing, since she was the one picking out the tree.

"How do we cut it down?" Aidan asked, and Sharpe could see the boy had switched gears into his scientific mind and was already thinking about how they were just getting to the good stuff—chain saws.

"Emma, would you mind keeping an eye on Baloo? He's very well trained to sit and stay, but he's young yet, and there are just so many distractions in the woods.

"Did you bring your safety glasses and gloves?" he asked Aidan.

Aidan grinned and pulled the glasses and gloves from his jean-jacket pocket. Sharpe moved over to the horses and returned with his own safety glasses and gloves, then explained how to safely rev up the chain saw and how to properly cut down a tree. Sharpe had given the lecture hundreds of times, but rarely to such an enthusiastic audience. Or maybe it was that he knew Aidan so well that he could read the fascination and curiosity in the boy's eyes.

Sharpe showed Aidan where he should start the cut and then carefully passed the chain saw on to Aidan, watching with pride as he cut through. Sharpe held the top of the tree, putting pressure on it so it would fall the right direction.

"Don't forget to call out *timber*," he reminded Aidan when the boy was close to felling the tree.

Aidan paused a moment and then yelled,

"Timber!" as the tree crashed to the ground right where Sharpe had anticipated it would.

He'd hoped maybe he'd have time to talk to Emma about what had happened with Bryan while they were tying up the tree for Rocky to drag back, but the moment passed with Aidan chattering on nonstop, reminding Sharpe of a baby bird in the spring. He wondered if this would be the right time to gift Baloo to Aidan, but he still didn't know if Aidan was even aware of the upcoming move to California, and he didn't want to say anything until he'd spoken to Emma about it.

They headed back toward the farm, and from that point on, he had to keep his attention on his horse and dragging the tree without having it get caught up on anything. He shoved his frustration to the back of his heart, determined to speak to her later. Surely she'd make time for him sometime this afternoon. Or maybe her heart was hurting too much to be able to talk about it at all. He couldn't help but be worried about her.

When they reached the farm, they loaded the tree into Sharpe's truck and made the short drive to Nan's house. They'd planned it so Gramps had Nan out for the afternoon while they set up and decorated the tree.

"Is it okay for Baloo to come inside the house?" Sharpe asked as they approached, tree in hand.

"Nan loves dogs. She's had a few of her own over the years," Emma replied, then pointed toward the front window. "We're going to put it up right here. This is going to be so pretty. Nan will be overjoyed."

Together, the three of them set up the tree, and then Emma directed Sharpe and Aidan as to where to find the lights and decorations. Despite Sharpe wondering why Emma was being so tight-lipped about what had happened the previous evening, he found himself becoming lost in the beauty of working together with Emma and Aidan to decorate the tree, wrapping multicolored strings of lights around the branches and then decorating them with red and silver bulb ornaments and gold ribbon covered with musical notes.

It almost felt as if they were a family. He wondered if Emma and Aidan were feeling the same way—connected. Blessed.

When they were finished decorating, Sharpe texted Gramps and told him it was time to bring Nan home. They couldn't have been too far away, because they walked in the door five minutes later, their canes thumping against the hardwood floor.

"Oh, my stars," Nan exclaimed when she saw the glittering tree. She pressed a hand to her throat, and tears sparkled in her eyes. "It's so beautiful. It's been years since I've had a tree. Living alone, it just didn't seem worth it to go through all that effort. But now, with you all here, I'm just so filled with gratitude my heart is about to burst."

Sharpe's gut tightened. With all of them there? Apparently she didn't know she would once again be living alone, though he expected it wouldn't be too long before Gramps and Nan tied the knot.

Then she wouldn't be alone anymore.

Too bad he didn't have a similar solution. His heart was already a big, gaping, empty wound.

"I spoke with Nan this morning about something very important. Though she has a lot of wonderful things going on in her life, she's agreed to allow Aidan and me to stay with her until we find a house of our own."

Sharpe's heart jumped and started pounding in his chest, and he strode to Emma and grasped both of her hands in his. "What are you saying?"

"That meeting with my attorney last night? It was to let me know he'd discovered an additional bank account in my mother's name. It was well hidden, as my father had put everything else in his name alone and had named Aidan as his sole beneficiary. Which is fine. It's what I want.

"However, my mother evidently somehow put aside money in her own account, one my dad knew nothing about. She'd been funneling money into it for years. And—" Emma paused as her voice took on a husky tone "—she listed me as the sole beneficiary."

Sharpe knew he was grinning so hard it might scare others away, but he didn't care. In his mind, he was putting two and two together, and if it made four, as he suspected it would...

"It's enough for you to start your business?" His own voice cracked with emotion. "And...and stay here with me?"

"I'll be putting in an offer for the shop you showed me at the real-estate office on Monday. I'm already thinking about what I'd like my logo to be. Maybe a steaming mug of coffee with—"

Sharpe whooped and grabbed her around the waist, swinging her round and round until she was dizzy. She threw back her head and laughed.

"Thank You, Jesus. Thank You, Jesus," Sharpe kept repeating. "He answered my prayer."

"Mine, too," Emma affirmed as Sharpe brought his lips down on hers.

"Ew," Aidan protested. "Do you have to do that here?"

Sharpe roared with laughter. "I think you'd better get used to me kissing your sister, because it's going to be happening a lot now."

Aidan made a face.

"Well, if it makes you feel better, I have a surprise for you today. Kind of an early Christmas gift."

"A present?" Aidan exclaimed. "What is it?"

Emma was beaming as Sharpe called Baloo to his side.

"Over the past few weeks, you've been working very hard with Baloo. Everyone who sees you knows what a great team you make.

I was thinking this might be a good time to make your team permanent."

For a moment, Aidan's gaze was full of excitement, but then it flooded with confusion, as if he didn't dare believe what Sharpe was trying to tell him. Given what Sharpe knew of Aidan's background, he supposed he wasn't really surprised.

He needed to be more specific.

"Baloo is your dog now," he said with a grin. "If you promise to take good care of him."

"You know I will," Aidan exclaimed. "Did you hear that, Baloo? You and I are a team now." He turned to Emma. "Can I go outside in the back and play with Baloo?"

"I think that's an excellent idea," Emma said, tenderly brushing back the boy's hair. "We'll talk about all the chores you'll have to do for him later."

The boy and his dog made a noisy exit, and Gramps and Nan seemed to have found somewhere else to be, leaving Sharpe and Emma alone in the room.

"I was waiting for you to call last night," he admitted, framing her face with one hand. "Why didn't you tell me?"

"I was going to. I picked up my phone a dozen times but then decided I really wanted to surprise you."

"Well, you did that. And you also almost split my heart in two."

"I'm sorry. I wanted to work our living situation out with Nan first. To be honest, I'm still in shock. I know the Bible says if you have the faith of a mustard seed, you can move mountains, but I don't think I even have that much faith. I was praying so hard that I wouldn't have to go back to my old job, that I'd be able to stay here and pursue a relationship with you, but I'm not sure I ever really believed there was any way that could become my reality. I feel as if I need to pinch myself."

"What can I do to prove to you that your reality is right in front of you? That he cares for you more than you can possibly imagine?" With every word he spoke, he lowered his head closer and closer to hers.

"Maybe," she said, pressing her lips to his, "a kiss is better than a pinch. I'd feel it all the way down to my heart."

"If one kiss is good, a dozen kisses are better," he agreed. "My heart is yours, Emma Fitzpatrick. I hope you know that."

"And mine belongs to you," Emma responded, laying her head on his chest and inhaling deeply. "Whoever would have thought when I first came here that I'd meet a surly cowboy who would steal my heart?"

"I didn't exactly think the fashionista who was wearing high heels to a country carnival would be my type. I guess God knows much better than we do, to have worked things out as He did. I thought my circumstances had me stuck in Whispering Pines. Now I know it was to meet you."

"And as for me, I'm standing here watching all my dreams come true," she said, squeezing him tight. "My brother. My business. And most of all, you. You've given me a reason to stay."

Epilogue

Four months later

Emma stared at her reflection in the mirror, admiring her fashionable outfit, complete with high heels. This used to be her everyday wear, but she hadn't put on heels in months, and she actually felt a little wobbly. She'd become used to the more casual clothes typical of mountain living.

But today was a special day, and she wanted to do something beyond the norm. This was a day she would remember all her life, one of many that had happened lately. She was in a serious relationship with Sharpe, and with every passing day, she was more and more certain he was the one. Aidan was excelling in school, both in grades and in sports, and he still worked for Sharpe on Saturdays. He and Baloo had become an amazing team, and the dog never left Aidan's side. A couple of times a month, she, Sharpe and Aidan visited Mongoose's shelter, and they volunteered at local hospitals whenever time permitted.

She heard the sound of Sharpe's truck pulling up in front of Nan's house. She was still trying to find a new place for her and Aidan to live, because Gramps wanted to move in with Nan when they married in May. She'd thought Sharpe might help her with that, but he'd seemed oddly distant whenever the subject came up.

"Wow," he said, taking a step back when she opened the door. "Don't you look stunning."

She smiled at the love of her life. That had been the reaction she'd been seeking.

"Is Aidan ready?"

"I don't know. Aidan?" she called down the hall, and Aidan appeared with Baloo at his heel. He was dressed country casual, with his cowboy hat and jean jacket, but that was fine with Emma, as that was exactly what the boy had assimilated into.

They climbed in the truck, and Sharpe

took them to their destination—a newly refurbished shop in the middle of the main thoroughfare. Even before she exited the truck, she admired the sparkling-clean windows and the logo, a steaming hot mug of coffee. Just above that were the words *The Coffee Lady Café*.

It was perfect. It had taken her several months to find and hire contractors and to set up her business and hire employees, but she was ready for this grand opening. She'd waited her whole life for this.

She was amazed by the number of people surrounding the café. It looked as if the whole town had come out to see the ribbon cutting, which Sharpe had arranged. She saw every Winslow in the crowd, along with their families, but of course they'd be there to support her. That was one thing she was learning about having an extended family—they were always there for her.

Sharpe reached for her hand. "Are you ready?"

"As I'll ever be. Maybe you should pinch me to let me know this is real."

"Now, you know what happens when you suggest that. I end up kissing you." He flashed her a toothy grin. "We'd better wait until later for that."

"Okay, then. Let's go cut the ribbon."

Sharpe lifted the oversize scissors, and his smile widened.

As they approached the front of the shop, the crowd's talk turned to applause. She suddenly realized they probably wanted some sort of speech, but she didn't have one prepared, so she decided to wing it.

"Thank you all so much for coming out to support me today. As most of you know, owning a business has been a dream of mine for many years. Now, with Sharpe's and the town's support, today I'm making my dream a reality."

There was more applause, and then Sharpe handed the scissors to her. "Make sure you cut right next to the bow," he suggested, "so the ribbon drops equally in half."

She stepped forward and positioned the scissors, but then she stopped as she saw something glittering from the ribbon's bow.

She looked closer, and then up at Sharpe, tears stinging her eyes.

With a tender smile, Sharpe untied the diamond solitaire ring and dropped to one knee before her.

"I don't want to eclipse what you've accomplished here today, but I can't wait any longer to tell you how much you mean to me. I didn't even know what I was missing until you and Aidan walked into my life, and now I can't imagine living without you. I love you with my whole heart and want to show you how much every day for the rest of our lives. Emma Fitzpatrick, will you be my wife?"

Her heart pounded, zinging around inside her like fireworks on the Fourth of July. She couldn't find the words.

"Don't leave me hanging here," Sharpe whispered.

"Of course, yes. Yes, yes, yes." Now that she'd found her voice, she didn't want to stop repeating the word. "I love you so much! There's nothing I want more than to be your wife." She paused. "But I think we should ask Aidan what he thinks. It's only fair."

"You think I'd propose in front of this many people if I didn't already know what Aidan thought of all this?"

As Sharpe stood and slid the ring on Emma's finger, Aidan appeared by their side and high-fived Sharpe. "This is so awesome," he exclaimed. "Now I get to hang out with Sharpe all the time."

Emma chuckled. Well, that was one way of looking at it.

Baloo barked, and Aidan gestured to the dog, who performed a backflip and then continued barking.

"Wow," Emma said. "When did he learn how to do that?"

"I just taught him that," Aidan answered. "To celebrate you and Sharpe getting married."

She picked up the scissors she'd dropped in a daze when Sharpe had proposed to her. "In the past few months, I've gone from being a single woman to discovering I have a brother and becoming his guardian, and now I have a family. I never, ever believed I could be blessed like this. So, that said, I don't think I ought to be the only one cutting this ribbon. My dream belongs to all three of us."

Sharpe stood on one side of Emma, and Aidan stood on the other. They each grabbed part of the scissors handle and deftly snipped at the ribbon, causing it to float to the ground. The crowd around them hadn't stopped applauding since she'd first approached the ribbon, and now it was even louder.

Her future was in front of her, beside her and all around her. She met Sharpe's eyes, which were brimming with love for her, and the two of them smiled before he tilted her chin up and pressed his lips to hers.

"I love you, Emma, now and forever."

She curled her fingers into his dark hair and kissed him back with all her heart.

* * * * *

Dear Reader,

After several books about the Winslow sisters, we're finally moving into the brothers' stories. How exciting is that?

Sharpe Winslow is as edgy as his name, and with good reason. He's emotionally closed down because so many people have left him in the past—his parents, his grandmother and his best friend, among others. He doesn't trust anyone to stay, especially not for him.

Emma Fitzpatrick is only visiting Whispering Pines with the younger brother she didn't even know she had but whom she is now guardian of. Her whole world is in a tailspin, but one thing she knows for sure—she isn't staying in this small town. Her whole life is waiting for her back in Los Angeles.

Both Sharpe and Emma are struggling to reconcile themselves to their loneliness. And that's the thing, I think. You don't have to be totally isolated to feel lonely. That may happen just as easily in a crowd of people. Have you ever felt this way?

I'm grateful we have a Savior who never

leaves or forsakes us. He took our loneliness with Him onto the cross.

I wish you every blessing and pray for you daily. Visit me at debkastnerbooks.com if you like.

Dare to Dream!
Deb Kastner

COMING NEXT MONTH FROM
Love Inspired

AN AMISH PROPOSAL FOR CHRISTMAS
Indiana Amish Market • by Vannetta Chapman

Assistant store manager Rebecca Yoder is determined to see the world and put Shipshewana, Indiana, behind her. The only thing standing in her way is training new hire Gideon Fisher and convincing him the job's a dream. But will he delay her exit or convince her to stay?

HER SURPRISE CHRISTMAS COURTSHIP
Seven Amish Sisters • by Emma Miller

Millie Koffman dreams of becoming a wife and mother someday. But because of her plus size, she doubts it will ever come true—especially not with handsome neighbor Elden Yoder. But when Elden shows interest in her, Millie's convinced it's a ruse. Can she learn to love herself before she loses the man loves?

THE VETERAN'S HOLIDAY HOME
K-9 Companions • by Lee Tobin McClain

After a battlefield incident leaves him injured and unable to serve, veteran Jason Smith resolves to spend his life guiding troubled boys with the help of his mastiff, Titan. Finding the perfect opportunity at the school Bright Tomorrows means working with his late brother's widow, principal Ashley Green...*if* they can let go of the past.

JOURNEY TO FORGIVENESS
Shepherd's Creek • by Danica Favorite

Inheriting failing horse stables from her estranged father forces Josie Shepherd to return home and face her past—including her ex-love. More than anything, Brady King fervently regrets ever hurting Josie. Could saving the stables together finally bring peace to them—and maybe something more?

THE BABY'S CHRISTMAS BLESSING
by Meghann Whistler

Back on Cape Cod after an eleven-year absence, Steve Weston is desperate for a nanny to help care for his newborn nephew. When the lone candidate turns out to be Chloe Richardson, the woman whose heart he shattered when they were teens, he'll have to choose between following his heart or keeping his secrets...

SECOND CHANCE CHRISTMAS
by Betsy St. Amant

Blake Bryant left small-town life behind him with no intention of going back—until he discovers the niece he never knew about is living in a group foster home. But returning to Tulip Mound also involves seeing Charlie Bussey, the woman who rejected him years ago. Can he open his heart enough to let them both in?

LICNM0822